PYRAMID

THE IRON TOMB

HUNTERS

KEEP UP WITH THE HUNT

Pyramid Hunters #2
Bones of the Sun God

PETER

PYRA

THE IR

HUNT

ALADDIN   NEW YORK   LONDON

VEGAS

AMID

ON TOMB

TERS

TORONTO   SYDNEY   NEW DELHI

This book is a work of fiction. Any references to historical events, real people, or real places are used fictitiously. Other names, characters, places, and events are products of the author's imagination, and any resemblance to actual events or places or persons, living or dead, is entirely coincidental.

ALADDIN

An imprint of Simon & Schuster Children's Publishing Division

1230 Avenue of the Americas, New York, NY 10020

First Aladdin paperback edition August 2017

Text copyright © 2016 by Peter Vegas

Cover illustration copyright © 2016 by Nigel Quarless

Interior illustrations on pages 1, 10, 32, 37, 70, 90, 108, 164, 192, 221, and 248 copyright © 2016 by Mohammad Aram; interior illustrations on pages 42, 43, 96, 100, 124, 151, 159, 195, 205, 207, 241, and 243 copyright © 2016 by Simon & Schuster, Inc.; map on page 77 copyright © 2016 by Shutterstock/zju; submarine on page 296 copyright © 2016 by Shutterstock/Gino Caron; ark illustraion on page 224 copyright © 2016 by iStockphoto

Also available in an Aladdin hardcover edition.

All rights reserved, including the right of reproduction in whole or in part in any form.

ALADDIN and related logo are registered trademarks of Simon & Schuster, Inc.

For information about special discounts for bulk purchases, please contact Simon & Schuster Special Sales at 1-866-506-1949 or business@simonandschuster.com.

The Simon & Schuster Speakers Bureau can bring authors to your live event.

For more information or to book an event contact the Simon & Schuster Speakers Bureau at 1-866-248-3049 or visit our website at www.simonspeakers.com.

Designed by Karin Paprocki

The text of this book was set in Bembo Standard.

Manufactured in the United States of America 0617 OFF

2 4 6 8 10 9 7 5 3 1

The Library of Congress has cataloged the hardcover edition as follows:

Names: Vegas, Peter, 1968- author.

Title: The Iron Tomb / Peter Vegas.

Description: First Aladdin hardcover edition. | New York : Aladdin, 2016. | Series: Pyramid hunters ; 1 | Summary: "Following the various clues his uncle left behind, using the same knowledge of Ancient Egyptian history, culture, and religion he once hated, Sam makes his way across Egypt trying to solve the mystery of his uncle's disappearance and, eventually, the secret of the Iron Tomb"—Provided by publisher.

Identifiers: LCCN 2015043253 (print) | LCCN 2016019389 (eBook) | ISBN 9781481445788 (hardcover) | ISBN 9781481445801 (eBook) |

Subjects: | CYAC: Mystery and detective stories. | Adventure and adventurers—Fiction. | Missing persons—Fiction. | Uncles—Fiction. | Egypt—Civilization—To 332 B.C.—Fiction. | Egypt—Fiction. | BISAC: JUVENILE FICTION / Action & Adventure / General. | JUVENILE FICTION / Mysteries & Detective Stories. | JUVENILE FICTION / People & Places / Africa.

Classification: LCC PZ7.1.V44 Ir 2016 (print) | LCC PZ7.1.V44 (eBook) | DDC [Fic]—dc23

ISBN 9781481445795 (pbk)

THE HUMAN THIGHBONE WAS THE wrong tool. Sam had worked that out pretty fast, stuck on his stomach in the cramped confines of the badly made tunnel. The idea had been to use it to sweep away the sand that had seeped in over the years, but it was too long and chunky for such a delicate job. The first time Sam accidentally hit one of the pieces of packing crate that had been used to shore up the walls and roof, he triggered a miniature waterfall of sand.

What he should have brought was something thinner, easier to handle. What really sucked was he could have. There had been a whole skeleton to choose from. But it was too late now, and it looked like the decision would be the last mistake Sam would ever make.

Sam's second to last mistake had been entering the aging tunnel in the first place. But he reminded himself that he was going to die anyway. At least this way he'd go out trying to escape.

As Sam pushed the ever growing mounds of sand out of the way with his bone spade, the tunnel creaked and groaned. Protestations of old age coupled with the indignation at having been invaded after so long.

A narrow path opened up, but already the sand was raining down, greedily claiming back the empty space. Sam tried to slither forward, but couldn't. His body was paralyzed from the waist down. While he'd been focused on the work in front of him, the tunnel had conspired to trap him from behind. Sand, flowing in silently through the new wounds Sam's trespassing had opened up, had buried his lower half in a warm cocoon. He tried to kick free. It was like swimming in concrete. His attempts became more frantic as panic took hold. Then, without warning, the physical effort paid off as one leg erupted from the mound.

It seemed Sam had been wrong about the thighbone. That wasn't the last mistake he'd ever make. Kicking was.

His leg's bid for freedom ended when it smashed into the roof. The loud *crack* that followed signaled the beginning of the end.

Sam twisted, desperate for a look at the damage

behind him. As he did, a plank of wood above gave way. Powered by hundreds of tons of desert sand, it crashed down onto his head. The miniature waterfalls became one horrendous downpour, and Sam's world went black.

Five days earlier

1

BUMS ON SEATS

"YOUR PHARAOH HAS A BIG BUM," SAID THE girl in 18B.

Sam stopped sketching, but he didn't look up. He had a few rules for plane trips. Actually, he had three:

Always order the chicken.

Always try for two cans of Coke when the drinks cart rolled by.

And, most important:

Always avoid conversation with the person in the seat next to him.

Sam had survived the eight-hour flight from New York to London without one word passing between him and the elderly Indian man next to him. He had also enjoyed a semi-dehydrated chicken breast, stuffed with something orange that the menu claimed was an apricot, and four cans of Coke. The second leg of the journey was the four-hour flight to Cairo. They'd made it just over halfway before the girl finally spoke.

Sam had been happy when he first saw her. He had just taken his seat when a huge Egyptian man began stuffing his backpack into the overhead locker above Sam's head. He wasn't fat, just really, *really* big. Big, like a professional wrestler or scary bodyguard for some sheikh. That, Sam thought, wasn't out of the question, seeing as the flight was heading to the Middle East.

Spillover was one of the many downsides to flying in the cramped confines of economy class. Sam shuddered at the thought of losing half his seat to the fleshy overflow of the man mountain next to him. The only upside was that he didn't look like much of a talker. But Sam was still relieved when a girl with shoulder length brown hair, who looked about thirteen—his age too—squeezed past the giant Egyptian and slid into seat 18B.

Now, two hours into the flight, she went and wrecked everything by speaking.

It wasn't that Sam was antisocial or had a problem with girls, he just hadn't hung out with many. That was one of the downsides of being at St. Albans, the all-boys boarding school he attended in Boston.

Girls weren't a completely unknown quantity. There were girls in the mixed rowing team he was part of, and sometimes, after practice on a Saturday, they'd all go out for a pizza or a movie. The outings were always supervised by one of the dorm teachers, but on those Saturday nights he could almost imagine what it was like to go to a normal school, where he would talk to girls on a daily basis. But he'd never pictured it happening at thirty thousand feet.

From the snippets of conversation Sam had heard between the girl and the air hostess, she sounded friendly enough. Under normal circumstances Sam imagined they could probably find stuff to talk about.

But it wasn't normal circumstances. They were on a plane.

Sam worked out pretty quickly that his aversion to airplane small talk was a direct result of the fact that he was always traveling alone. The person who ended up seated next to him would see a thirteen-year-old by himself and assume he was feeling lonely, perhaps a little nervous, and could do with a friend on the long flight ahead. It would start with a cheerful introduction and then, because they were on a plane, there would be an inquiry about Sam's destination. From there it was only a matter of time until the conversation led to questions about the whereabouts of Sam's parents. And therein was the problem: Sam was sick and tired of telling strangers about his parents. Instead, he had come up with several techniques to kill such a conversation before it could start.

Pretending to sleep was the simplest and the most effective. Unfortunately, it meant he almost missed out on the free Cokes and chicken, so he used this only in extreme situations.

Headphones on, music up, and a blank stare out the window worked well, but Sam's favorite method was to pull out his sketch pad and start drawing. Given that this was how he spent a lot of his spare time after school, it wasn't hard at all, and half the time it also helped him forget he was crammed on an airplane in the first place.

Sam liked to draw. He found it easy to tune out everything except the lines he was making on the page. When he combined this with his headphones, it was almost guaranteed to prevent fellow travelers from trying to break the ice. Unfortunately for Sam, this time his drawing had worked against him.

Only a few seconds had passed since the girl's comment on his pharaoh's rear end, but the clock was ticking, and the gap would soon become an awkward silence. He couldn't avoid conversation without looking like a weirdo, so Sam scrambled for a response that acknowledged her comment without opening the door to a full-blown conversation.

But before he could speak, the girl jumped back in again.

"With a bum like that he definitely wouldn't be sitting in one of these seats," she said, thumping the armrest between them. "He'd be up front in business class, don't you think?"

Sam nodded and couldn't help smiling. "I bet that guy sitting behind you wishes he was up in business," he whispered, nodding toward the man. "It'll probably take a couple of air hostesses to pull him out of his seat."

"You mean Bassem," said the girl, glancing over her shoulder.

Sam's face dropped. "I . . . I didn't realize you were traveling with him," he offered apologetically. But if he expected her to take offense, he was mistaken.

The girl laughed. "Believe it or not," she said, her voice rising, "he's one of the smallest in his family. Aren't you, Bassem?"

Sam cringed as the girl turned to face the Egyptian giant, but the man didn't move. He'd had his face buried in a book since takeoff and he either didn't hear the girl or had chosen to ignore her.

She turned back to Sam, unfazed by the lack of

response. "Bassem's not big on talking . . . just *big*. I'm Mary, by the way." She stuck out her hand. "And you're Sam Force."

"How did you know that?"

Mary pointed to the small, crumpled piece of paper lying next to the two empty Coke cans on Sam's tray. "It's on your boarding pass."

"Oh."

"So why are you off to Cairo, Sam Force? Searching for big-bummed pharaohs?"

Here we go, thought Sam, regretting that he'd slipped up on his "no chat" rule. "Nothing that exciting," he mumbled. "My uncle lives there. He's an Egyptologist. I have to spend the summer with him."

"You don't seem too thrilled."

That was putting it mildly. For five summers Sam had traveled to Egypt to stay with his uncle Jasper, a man of weird words and whiskers. At first it had all been a bit of an adventure. It had held the promise of discovering ancient tombs, mummies, and chests full of treasure. But the reality was quite different. Sam's summer tended to involve a lot of time spent sitting in tents, sifting through piles of rocks, looking for bits of pottery. Trouble was, old bits of pottery look a lot like small rocks, and that makes the whole process very time consuming and incredibly boring.

Sam was thirteen now, and in the past couple of years the long, hot days in the desert had lost their allure. He wanted to have a normal vacation, doing the kinds of things other kids in his class did. Going to the movies, swimming, and hanging out with friends. If there was going to be any sand involved, he wanted it to be on a beach. The thought of yet another summer wasted in the Egyptian desert bored him to tears.

Apparently it showed on his face.

"I'm not really into all that old Egyptian stuff," Sam said.

Mary laughed. "Well, I'm afraid you're heading to the wrong country, because pretty much everything in Egypt is Egyptian and old."

There was another reason Sam would never truly feel comfortable in Cairo. If he was honest with himself, it was the *real* reason he hated his summer vacation. Memories that he had spent five years trying to bury in his mind like unwanted artifacts. His school counselors tried to dig them up on purpose, and sometimes inquisitive travelers did it by accident.

Mary elbowed him in the ribs.

Sam started. "Sorry, what?"

"I was asking what your uncle is working on at the moment."

"Some old pharaoh."

Mary smiled. "Yes, well, they all tend to be pretty old. Any idea which one?"

"Akon something," Sam said as he pulled the copy of his uncle's last e-mail out of his pocket. "Akhenaten," he pronounced slowly.

"The heretic king."

Sam skimmed the first few lines of his uncle's e-mail. "Yeah, that's what my uncle called him. Are you into Egyptian stuff?"

Mary's eyes lit up. "Mad for it. I'm Egyptian, you know. Well, half, anyway."

Sam glanced back at the giant Egyptian with a book for a head, sitting behind her. "Is that your dad?"

Mary laughed again. "Bassem? No way. He's more like a . . . what would you say, Bassem, a minder?" Bassem lived up to his nontalkative reputation by keeping his nose buried in his book.

"My mother was Egyptian, and my father is English," continued Mary, "but my interest in Egyptology comes from him. It's a hobby for him, but I want it to be more than that for me. I'm going to be just like your uncle."

Sam rolled his eyes. "Trust me, you don't want to do that." But even as he spoke, a plan formed in his mind. "Mary, I don't suppose you could tell me a bit about this Akon guy?"

"Akhenaten? Sure. What do you want to know?"

"Not too much," Sam assured her. "Just the basics."

Mary tapped her chin with one finger, as though she were a professor pondering an important question. "Did you know that he got his name as the heretic king because he banned the worship of all the gods and decreed there would be only one? Aten, the sun god."

"Why did he do that?"

"I'm not sure. Make things a bit easier for his people, perhaps. There were more than five hundred different gods back then."

"Okay. What else?" Sam asked as he added a sun above his big-bummed pharaoh.

"There's a lot written on him. I bet your uncle has a few books."

Sam was sure he did, but that was what he wanted to avoid. "Can't you just tell me the important stuff?"

"Well, I'm not really an expert on him. Why are you so interested anyway? I thought you weren't into old Egyptian stuff."

Sam looked up from his sketchbook. "I'm not, but I really want to go to the new water park in Cairo."

She frowned. "I don't follow."

"Well, my uncle always likes me to do a bit of research on his current dig before I arrive. I never do. I just kind of fake my way through it. But if I turn up and impress him with all the stuff I learned on this Aken guy . . ."

"Akhenaten."

"Whatever. Then he might let me go to the water park."

"Let you?" said Mary. "Is your uncle some kind of tyrant?"

"No, not at all," said Sam. "It's just that he thinks I'm into all this ancient Egypt stuff as much as he is. He always sees my visits as a chance to teach me. He wants to pack in as much as he can. I've tried to drop hints about movies and trips to places that aren't the desert, but it's like he thinks I'm there for Egyptology School and not summer vacation."

"So you think that if you really impress him, he might be more inclined to grant you a special wish?"

Sam frowned. "Well, now you are making it sound kind of dumb, but yeah. That was the plan."

"So what's in it for me?"

"I dunno. You can come too, if you want."

"Sam Force, are you asking me on a date?"

Sam's face dropped. "What? No. Not like that. I just meant . . . you know . . ."

Mary laughed. "Relax, Force. I'm just messing with you. If I can help you impress your uncle enough to get you a trip to the water park, then that'll be my good deed for the summer. Now, for starters you're going to have to learn to say that Aken guy's name properly."

★ ★ ★

BY THE TIME THE FLIGHT LANDED, SAM
had scored two more cans of Coke and what felt like
a school year's worth of information on Akhenaten.
Mary had well and truly backed up her claim about
being "mad" on all things Egyptian. Sam knew he
wouldn't remember most of it, but hoped enough would
stick to impress his uncle.

After the Egyptian lessons, they had moved on to
other topics, and thankfully none of those had been
his parents.

They chatted about music, where they quickly
discovered they had totally different tastes. Sam was
into guitars, the louder the better, while Mary was into
dance music and listed half a dozen DJs Sam had never
heard of. Unable to find any common ground in music,
they moved on to movies. When the plane touched
down they were trying to rank the Harry Potter series
from best to worst, but had come to the conclusion it
was more a case of best to most awesome. For once,
the conversation had been easy and light. Mary never
pushed Sam for more personal information.

It never failed to amaze Sam how, within seconds of
hitting the runway, the calm and ordered interior of a
plane transformed into a writhing mass of bodies and
arms as everyone leapt to their feet and wrestled their

bags from the overhead lockers. Repeated requests from the cabin staff to remain seated were always ignored as the urge to be the first to get out the door swept through the plane like a virus.

Sam, as always, sat back to enjoy the show and was about to comment on the chaos when Mary's giant guardian plucked her from her seat to join the fray. As the river of passengers swallowed them up, Mary had time to manage only a quick smile and point to her seat. On it was a piece of paper with a note:

Good luck with Operation Waterpark.

Call me if you need more help.

Mary 555-7563.

When Sam looked up again, Mary had been lost in the flood of cheap shirts and Windbreakers.

THE MAD RUSH TO EXIT THE AIRCRAFT seemed even more comical when you knew you weren't even at the terminal. Like a lot of international airports, Cairo received more flights than it had room for, so many passengers found their plane parked in a distant corner of the runway and were forced to endure a bumpy bus ride that seemed to take almost as long as the flight itself.

Sam gave up all hope of catching up with Mary again when his bus stopped and disgorged him and forty others into a throng of more than five hundred people, all pushing toward the next challenge: the very limited number of customs desks.

The first time he had arrived in Cairo alone the process had been freaky, but after five summers, there was no longer any fear. Now it was just depressing. The wait in the long winding queue was tedious and a fitting intro to a vacation that promised nothing but more of the same.

After answering a series of questions from a customs official who seemed as unhappy about being there as he was, Sam collected his bag and slipped out through the automatic doors into the cavernous arrival hall. The sensation always reminded Sam of something he witnessed at a fish farm on a school trip: baby fish, being tipped from the relative safety of a bucket into a big blue lake. At Cairo airport, passengers were funneled out into a sea of brown faces sprinkled with sets of gleaming white teeth. Cries of "Taxi! Taxi!" rippled through the mob as each new potential customer, or *victim*, as Sam liked to think of them, appeared from behind the sliding doors.

Strolling calmly along the crowd barrier, Sam put on his best "been here, seen this" look, but despite his obvious disinterest, he still received a "Taxi! Taxi!" from every face he passed. He didn't take it personally, it was just how the place worked, and he really had seen it all before. After running the "Taxi! Taxi!" gauntlet he would reach the end of the crowd barrier, and standing there in a hideous Hawaiian shirt and old faded blue cap, with a face full of white whiskers, would be Uncle Jasper. After a rib-crushing hug, Jasper would grab Sam's bag and usher him to the door, swatting off "Taxi! Taxi!" related inquires as he went.

That was how it had always happened.

But not this time.

2
THE POLYESTER WALL

THE TRICK WAS TO KEEP MOVING. IF YOU stopped, even for a moment, the "Taxi! Taxi!" men would take it as a sign that you were contemplating their message. Then it was down to who would get the job. Closest man to the victim was the way that worked. In seconds you'd find yourself surrounded by a tightly packed group of drivers, all trying to grab a piece of you. Literally. The problem was, Sam had to stop. He was at the end of the crowd barriers. This was where Uncle Jasper always stood. Always.

The cries of "Taxi! Taxi!" were becoming more urgent as competition for Sam's business increased.

Eager hands grabbed for his bag, and as Sam wrenched it free, he scanned the crowd for a glimpse of a garish Hawaiian shirt. Instead, he was confronted by an ever shrinking circular wall of stinky polyester.

Suddenly, a smiling face topped with a mop of greasy black hair appeared at Sam's feet. Even by Cairo standards, tunneling between the legs of the other drivers was a cheeky move. Howls of protest rippled through the group as the teen forced his way to his feet. Sam's first thought was that he looked way too young to drive a taxi.

The boy leaned in close so he could make himself heard above the racket. "Your name is Sam, yes?"

Sam let out a sigh of relief. "Yes. Yes, it is. Did my uncle send you?"

"I know nothing of your uncle, but there is a man looking for you. He has your picture."

Sam was confused. "Okay. Maybe my uncle sent him. Can you take me to him?"

The boy shook his head. "No, my friend. This is not a man you want to see."

"Why not?"

"He is police. In this town, that is not good. Come, come." The young driver picked up Sam's suitcase and began burrowing through the crowd.

"Why are the police looking for me?" asked Sam, but

he already suspected it had something to do with his uncle. "You need to take me to him," he said more forcefully.

"No, no. You come with me," the boy insisted as he squeezed through a gap in the polyester wall. "It's better."

The faint trace of panic building in Sam since he'd gotten to the end of the crowd barriers now threatened to overwhelm him as he watched a complete stranger disappear with his gear. "Stop! Take me to the police," he shouted, lunging for his suitcase.

The mention of the P-word had a magical effect on the taxi drivers. They melted away in an instant, stepping away from both Sam and the rather surprised Egyptian boy who was holding the suitcase. Sam saw a flicker of worry in the boy's eyes, and he spun around to see a chubby, middle-aged man in a faded brown suit waddling toward them. "Is that the man who has my picture?" Sam turned back for an answer, but the boy had made like a taxi driver and disappeared, leaving the suitcase on the ground.

"Sam Force?" wheezed the man in the brown suit. "You are Sam Force, yes?"

"Yes, I am. Where's my uncle?"

The policeman either didn't hear Sam, or chose to ignore him. Wrapping a pudgy hand around the suitcase, he motioned toward the far end of the arrival hall. "Come with me, please."

★ ★ ★

SAM FOLLOWED THE POLICEMAN AND his bag through a door with a large sign that read AUTHORIZED PERSONNEL ONLY. They shuffled down a long white corridor, up two flights of stairs, and down another identical corridor. At the far end was their final destination: a small room with a battered steel table and two matching chairs.

"Please have a seat," said the policeman as he collapsed into his. The walk from the arrival hall had exhausted him. His forehead was covered in beads of sweat that sparkled like little jewels under the naked bulb hanging above the table. He made a show of flicking through the papers in the file that had been waiting there, but Sam suspected this was an excuse to get his breath back.

Minutes passed. The silence and the man's lack of urgency began to get to Sam. If it was some kind of interview technique, it was working. At first Sam had been glad to be free of the mad crush of taxi drivers and the insistent boy. He was with a policeman now. Everything would be all right. But the man in front of him was making no effort to reassure him. In fact, he was acting like he was barely aware that Sam was there.

Sam had been determined that he wouldn't be the first to speak, but he couldn't stand the silence. The fat man had won. "Where is my uncle?" He'd tried to deliver the question calmly, but he sounded like a whiny kid.

The policeman looked up from his file and smiled, but the act wasn't meant to offer comfort. "That," he sneered, "is what we were hoping you could help us with."

"What do you mean? I just arrived. I was supposed to meet Uncle Jasper here."

The cop closed the brown folder with a theatrical *thump*. "Yes, we are aware of that and had hoped to make contact with your uncle ourselves. But it seems he has decided not to show his face."

Sam's mind raced. "Why would he do that? I mean, maybe something is wrong. Maybe something happened to him."

"Something is wrong, all right." The policeman thumped the folder again to make his point. "Your uncle has disappeared, along with a great deal of his employer's money. A *great* deal of money," he repeated, then looked down at his notes. "And a metal detector."

"From the EEF?" Sam shook his head. "He took money from the EEF? They don't have any. That's the problem. My uncle is always complaining that his work is underfunded."

The policeman's eyes sparkled like the sweat on his forehead. He thrust a chubby hand inside his jacket for a pen. Throwing open the file, he began to scribble furiously. "I see. So you are saying your uncle has had money troubles with the EEF?"

Sam had a feeling things were getting out of control. "No . . . I mean, well, he works for them. The Egyptian Exploratory Fund . . . they fund his work. It's what they do!" Sam sat back and took a deep breath, aware that the policeman was writing what he was saying, word for word. "Listen," he said calmly. "My uncle wouldn't steal money. If you knew him, you'd know how stupid that idea is. He just wouldn't. There must be some mistake."

The policeman made a show of slipping his pen back into his pocket, as if to let Sam know he wasn't interested in his theories. "Young boy, the evidence speaks for itself, so perhaps I would say to you there are things you do not know about your uncle."

"What evidence?"

"You don't need to concern yourself with that. Now, before we conclude the interview, there is something you can help us with. We are having trouble locating your uncle's residence. It seems the EEF has no record of it." The pen was produced again, placed on the folder, and slid across the table. "If you would be so kind as to write down the address, then we can proceed with organizing your departure."

"Departure?"

"Naturally, you cannot stay in Egypt. Arrangements will be made to return you to your boarding school in Boston."

"But what about my uncle? You're not listening. My uncle wouldn't steal money. If he's disappeared, then he must be in trouble. You need to find him."

The policeman leaned across the table, a trace of menace tainting his tone as he spoke. "We will do everything necessary to find your uncle and bring him to justice. You can be sure of that."

"You've already decided he's guilty."

"He *is* guilty!" The policeman heaved himself to his feet. "Your uncle will be hunted down and put in jail for a very long time. Do you understand? Now give me his address." He rammed a chubby finger into the folder.

The sudden outburst caught Sam by surprise, and the fright must have showed on his face. The policeman smirked and lowered his considerable bulk back on his seat. He was about to say something else when he was interrupted by a polite knock.

"Excuse me, sir. Ahmed from the front desk needs to see you. Your car is about to be towed away."

Sam was in a daze, but the voice in the doorway registered somewhere in his brain. He looked up to see the boy who had tried to take his bag.

Muttering and cursing, the policeman pulled himself out of his chair again and waddled out of the room. He left without a backward glance, slamming and locking the door behind him. Sam was still trying to work out what had happened when the door opened again, and the smiling taxi driver slipped in.

The boy darted over to the suitcase. "I tell you, you do not want to speak to this man. You agree now, yes?"

"Um, I guess."

"So, I come get you. But we must hurry," the boy urged. "The policeman will be back soon."

It was Sam's turn to spring from his chair as the boy and suitcase disappeared out the door. "Is the policeman's car really being towed away?" he asked as they raced down the corridor.

"No," the boy answered over his shoulder. "I don't even think there is a front desk. So we need to hurry before that policeman finds out."

AS THEY CAME DOWN THE STAIRS, THE door that opened into the terminal seemed a long way off to Sam. Surely, the fat policeman would bust them before they made it out. The boy had reached the same conclusion. At the bottom of the staircase he slipped around behind Sam, motioning for him to follow.

"Come, come. We wait here."

"What's your name?" asked Sam as they squeezed into a space that made Harry Potter's bedroom look big.

"Hadi," he whispered.

"Why are you doing this?"

The door at the other end of the corridor opened.

"Quiet," hissed Hadi, pushing Sam's head down into the shadows behind the suitcase. The sound of shoes slapping on concrete got louder. Sam didn't need to see to know it was the policeman. It was probably the most exercise he'd had in years. The heavy footsteps and labored breathing faded as he climbed the stairs.

"Let's go, my friend," said Hadi. "The big man will discover you have gone very shortly."

That thought propelled Sam out of their hiding place, and he led the way toward the door. He grabbed the door handle and pulled. It didn't move, and his panic must have shown.

"Push," said Hadi calmly. "And do not rush. We don't want to draw attention."

Sam's heart was beating so fast it felt like it was going to burst out of his mouth. He took a deep breath, pushed the door open, and stepped out into the bustling terminal. The gaggle of "Taxi! Taxi!" chanters had formed around the arrival gate again. Nobody gave the two boys wandering toward the main doors a second glance, but it still took all Sam's self-control not to break into a run. Hadi must have sensed this, because he spoke softly from behind. "Slowly, slowly, my friend. We have plenty of time. The fat man is far behind us."

The airport's cool air dissolved as the sliding glass doors parted for the boys, and they were engulfed by the hot, humid Cairo summer. Hadi took the lead now, crossing the road into the huge airport parking lot. As they moved deeper into the sea of dusty late-model cars, Sam couldn't help checking over his shoulder for a sign that they were being pursued.

The third time he did it, he walked straight into Hadi, who had stopped next to a battered old purple Skoda. Nearly every taxi in Cairo looks like it had just taken part in a demolition derby, but they all had the same color scheme—and it wasn't purple.

"I thought you were a taxi driver," Sam said as Hadi tossed the suitcase into the trunk.

The boy shrugged. "I drive. People pay money. That makes me a taxi driver, yes?"

"Fair enough. But why go to all that trouble to help me?"

Hadi opened the passenger door for Sam. "I don't like the police. They make much trouble for everyone.

That man with your picture, I know he is police straightaway, so when I see you, I decide to make a little trouble for him."

"Lucky for me."

"And maybe lucky for me if you decide to reward me." Hadi beamed a choirboy smile as he shut Sam's door and skipped around to the driver's side.

IT SEEMED ODD TO SAM THAT AFTER GOING to all the trouble of getting him out of the airport, Hadi was going to kill him before he got paid. But that was how things looked as the young Egyptian coaxed the Skoda to a crazy speed down the main road into the city.

Hadi swerved from lane to lane, hunting the empty spaces between cars and trucks or making his own by nudging his car across the painted line and forcing the driver next to him to brake.

Sam thought their mad dash was over when they caught up to two huge trucks blocking both city-bound lanes. Hadi thumped his horn impatiently as he raced up behind them, like an angry dog harassing two lumbering elephants. One of the trucks drifted out of its lane, and a narrow gap appeared, but it was too small for the Skoda. Or so Sam thought.

He watched wide-eyed as Hadi slotted his car in

between the moving walls of steel with just inches to spare. The stereo roar of truck engines drowned out the sound of Hadi's horn as they raced up the truck canyon. Sam gripped the faded old dashboard so hard that cracks appeared around his fingers. The gap of sunlight ahead shrank alarmingly, but just as Sam readied himself for the screech of metal on metal they popped out onto open road.

"How long have you been driving?" Sam forced out through gritted teeth.

"Many years," Hadi replied with a beaming smile. "I drive good, yes? That is why all my clients like me. Fast man around town."

Sam was surprised Hadi would ever get a repeat customer. Any trip in a Cairo taxi was like a turn on the bumper cars, but Hadi was taking the experience to a whole new level.

"Sit back, my friend. Relax!"

Sam suspected that Hadi was more concerned about the damage being done to the dashboard than his comfort, but he reluctantly eased his grip and sank back into his seat.

"You see that," said Hadi, pointing at a small pendant swinging wildly from the rearview mirror.

"That is scarab beetle. It is good luck and will keep us safe." As if to prove this theory, he gunned

the Skoda into another impossibly tight gap, this time between two buses.

"You sure one is enough?"

Hadi's laugh was punctuated by the synchronized blasts of two bus horns. "You are a funny guy," he said.

Sam wanted to smile, but his attention quickly returned to his imminent death as the Skoda bore down on its next target: a truck loaded with goats.

"So, where do you want to go?" asked Hadi as he honked impatiently.

"Do you know Mitre Tower?"

"Next to the old souk? Yes. I live nearby. But if the police know your uncle lives there, it may not be safe."

"They don't."

"Excellent. I will have you there in no time, my friend."

"No rush," said Sam. And he meant it.

3

CATS AND COCKROACHES

THE DROP-OFF WAS SHORT AND SWEET.

When the battered old Skoda departed in a cloud of smoke, Sam was twenty US dollars lighter in the pocket. It was nearly half the cash he had, but Sam thought Hadi deserved it. Not only for the help getting him out of the airport, but also for getting him to Mitre Tower alive.

As he rode the elevator to the seventeenth floor, Sam allowed himself to entertain a small glimmer of hope. There was still a chance his uncle was hiding at his apartment until he had sorted out the mess with the police. But as he stood in front of the door and the echoes of his knocking faded away, so did the hope.

He dumped his bag and pulled the crumpled e-mail from his pocket. Printing it out had been just a precaution, but as he reread the oddly worded note, he wondered if his uncle had had a premonition of the trouble that was to come.

From: Jasper Force j.force@eef.com

Date: Monday, July 20, 2015 at 10:45 AM

To: s.force@stalbans.com

My Sam,

Prepared for another summer of sun and sand? Research has taken me to Alexandria of late, where I am delving into the heretical past of Akhenaten. The controversial eighteenth-dynasty pharaoh. I plan to ship out shortly and barring any unforeseen holdups, I will be back in Cairo by Saturday to greet you at the airport. But prepare for any eventuality—that's always been my motto—and so, in the unlikely event there is some kind of holdup or we miss each other, then this note will help. Simply line up at the door to gain access to my palace.

Uncle Jasper loved creating codes and puzzles for Sam to work out. On his last vacation Sam had awoken to find a treasure map on his bed. His uncle had left for work, and a note told him that the map would lead him to a special treat. *X* turned out to mark the spot of a movie theater, and Sam was stoked—until he got inside and discovered the movie was a documentary about Bast, the Egyptian cat god.

So, here he was again with another puzzle that no doubt contained some kind of educational twist. The only difference was Sam was in no mood for stupid games. It was late, he was tired, his uncle was missing, and he had just escaped from police custody. These thoughts began to bounce around his mind, agitating, demanding attention. But he refused to give in to them. That wouldn't solve anything. Instead, Sam slammed the door on his worries and focused on getting through the one right in front of him.

The last line made the least sense: . . . *this note will help. Simply line up at the door to gain access to my palace.* It was odd, even for Jasper. Sam glanced around the dimly lit corridor. Line up where? At the door? Sam presumed the reference to "my palace" was Jasper's apartment. Plenty of creative license there, calling a poky one-bedroom hovel a palace. The building was more than thirty years old and in desperate need of repair. But so was a lot of Cairo.

The faded and cracked white tiles that lined the walls of the corridor made the place feel like an old hospital. Perhaps in an effort to avoid this comparison, the owners had added tiles with hand-painted pictures of ancient Egyptian gods. They must have cost a bit more, because they had been used sparingly, spaced out at door handle height every few feet. The one beside the door to Jasper's apartment featured a spooky sitting black cat.

Sam stared at the cat. The cat stared back. Sam recognized the ancient feline from the documentary his uncle had made him watch. It was Bast. He glanced down at the e-mail again. *Simply line up.*

The answer was right there on the page in front of him. The first letter on each line formed the message: Pat Bast.

Sam reached out and placed his hand on the Bast tile. It was loose; the grouting around the edge had been chipped away. By digging his fingers into the edges, he was able to pull the tile out of the wall. Behind it a hole the size of a matchbox had been chipped into the concrete, and sitting inside was a small brass key.

Sam couldn't help grinning as he removed the key from its hiding place. He knew his uncle would be pleased at how quickly he'd solved the puzzle. After carefully returning the tile to its place in the wall, Sam let himself inside his uncle's home.

A first-time visitor to Uncle Jasper's apartment would have thought the place had been ransacked. But

Sam knew this was how it always looked. Jasper didn't believe in tidying up after himself—or hiring someone to do it.

Sam dropped his suitcase behind the door and collapsed into a chair at the small wooden table that marked the boundary between the tiny kitchen and the rest of the shoe box–sized room. As he sat there in the dark, the events of the past few hours finally closed in on him.

Why was this happening to him? He hadn't wanted to come back to this stupid city again. He thumped the table in frustration, and watched a piece of paper flutter off the table and slide across the floor. Old memories surged to the surface, thoughts he had worked hard to bury in the past few years, but in his exhausted state they were harder to push away. He'd been abandoned before, and this time, if his uncle was gone, that was it. There was no one else. That was why he'd run when Hadi had offered him the chance. To stay in that room with the police and be shipped home would have been throwing his fate into the hands of others. He was never going to let that happen again. His train of thought was a runaway now, and sleep loomed as the tantalizing solution to his trauma.

The journey to the bedroom was a few short steps. An easier, more comfortable option than the foldout couch he was normally assigned. Despite his state Sam's conscience nagged, telling him that now was no time to sleep. He consoled himself with the thought that he would be far more use to his uncle with a bit of rest. Just an hour, he told himself, and then he would make a plan. Before the aging mattress springs had finished groaning under his weight, the chatter of Sam's mind had come to an end, and he drifted off to sleep.

THE COCKROACH WAS ROBOTIC. A MARVEL of miniature engineering. The scraping sounds were coming from its spindly little legs as it scuttled up Sam's chest toward his face. There was relief, seconds later, when he woke to find it had been a dream, but that feeling vanished almost instantly as Sam realized that the noises his imaginary cockroach had been making were inspired by identical and very real sounds coming from the door to the apartment.

Someone was picking the lock.

Sam eased off the bed, slow enough not to make any noise, but aware he had only seconds to hide himself. As he did, he was thankful he'd been so exhausted he hadn't even gotten under the sheets. Sam could feel the thick layer of dust on the floorboards as he slid under the bed. There was a chance that whoever was trying to get in might not realize he was there. But at the same time Sam couldn't help thinking that hiding under the bed had to be the single most obvious hiding place in the history of obvious hiding places.

The bedroom door was ajar, and from his terrible hiding spot Sam watched the gap glow as light spilled in from the corridor. He saw a dark shape, then heard the front door click shut and darkness returned.

Sam's jaw locked so tight he could feel his teeth being forced back up into their gums. He tried to slow his breathing, conscious of any sound that might give him away, but at the same time listening intently for noises that could help form a picture of what was happening in the next room.

Shuffling feet, then the shuffling of books. The intruder was at the kitchen table. Sam swallowed—an almost impossible feat, given the tennis ball–sized lump in his throat. There was a *thud* as one of the books was dropped back onto the table. Then more shuffling of feet as they headed to the bedroom.

The door creaked as it was pushed open. Sam lay there, rigid with fear. In the moonlight he could just make out a pair of shiny black leather boots. They moved across the room until they were inches from his face; the tart smell of fresh polish filled his nostrils. Any second the boots would take a step back, a face would appear, and he'd be busted. But it didn't happen.

Instead, the boots turned and the intruder left the room, pulling the door closed behind him. There was more rustling of papers, more footsteps, then another *click*. Was that the front door? Sam allowed himself the luxury of a deep gulp of air, the first since he'd slipped under the bed. But he remained still, listening for any sign of danger.

Sam was convinced that the final sound had been the apartment door closing, but what if it was a trap? A trick to flush him out? His breathing, fast and raspy, sounded like an old steam train struggling up a hill. He shut his eyes and tried to calm himself. It worked too well. His shattered mind took it as an invitation to shut down, and once again he drifted off to sleep.

DESPITE THE DOUBLE-PANED WINDOWS, the horn symphony performed by Cairo's early morning traffic acted as Sam's wake-up call. Before his brain could remind him where he was and why, he tried to sit up and smacked his head on the frame of the bed. It was a sucker punch of a wake-up call and a rubbish way to start the day.

He moved slower the second time, and as he slid out from his hiding place, Sam spotted something else hidden under the bed: an envelope jammed between the mattress and the bed frame. His body was sore after a night on cold floorboards, and now his head throbbed, but that was forgotten as he sat on the bed and opened the envelope. Inside, he found a swipe card for his uncle's office and a small piece of paper. Sam's excitement turned to confusion as he looked at the strange scribbles. Slipping his new discoveries into his pocket, Sam got up and went to check the rest of the apartment.

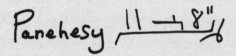

Uncle Jasper's home looked even worse in the harsh light of day, but none of that was the intruder's fault. In fact they'd tidied the place up. The books and papers that had been scattered across the kitchen table were gone, making it officially the cleanest surface in the place.

What was so important about the books? Sam tried to remember their titles, but he hadn't paid any attention to them. At the time he'd just wanted to rest his head somewhere. He played that moment over in his mind, and the image of a piece of paper sliding off the table came back to him.

He scanned the floor. The intruder had probably done the same thing, but Sam had the advantage of daylight. A small white triangle was sticking out from under the fridge. He grabbed the piece of paper and wiped the dust off it, but like the one he'd found in the envelope, he had no idea what he was looking at.

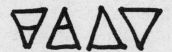

Two weird clues in as many minutes. It was like the start of another one of Uncle Jasper's educational adventures. But things were different this time. This was no game. His uncle was missing, and he was wanted by the police. Weren't things supposed to seem a bit better in the daylight?

As Sam sat at the kitchen table, the same script began to run in his head. How had he gotten into this mess? Twenty-four hours ago he had been preparing himself for another boring Egyptian vacation. Now he felt like he was fighting for his life. Maybe not his, but definitely his uncle's.

Besides the obscure clues, the swipe card to the EEF offices, and thirty bucks, Sam had little else going for him, and that made the other piece of paper in his pocket all the more important.

When Sam had taken Mary's number on the plane, he'd been thinking only about more ways she could help him with his water park plan, but everything had changed. Mary was his only friend in this weird town, and to find his uncle, he would need all the help he could get.

4

A BURGLAR
IS BORN

"SORRY ABOUT CALLING SO EARLY."

"No problem. I was up," Mary said, taking a sip of her chocolate milk. "If you hadn't called, Bassem would have made us go for a run, but I talked him into dropping me off here instead. I've got an hour before he'll be back to pick me up." She glanced out the window at the constant stream of cars. "I can never sleep in when I'm in Cairo. Don't you just love the hustle and bustle of this place?"

"Yeah," Sam lied.

On a normal vacation Sam would sleep in for as long as he could, but this morning he couldn't wait to get out of his uncle's apartment. It wasn't the "being alone" thing. It was the feeling that he wasn't doing anything to help his uncle. He'd paced the apartment until what he thought was a respectable hour, but eight a.m. was really only respectable if, like him, you'd been up since five thirty.

He and Mary had met downtown at a large McDonald's. Outside, hundreds of dusty vehicles clogged one of Cairo's chaotic streets. Inside, Mary picked up exactly where she'd left off on the plane: bright and cheerful and talking nonstop. For Sam, it felt like the plane trip had been another life. Things had changed beyond belief in the short time since they'd seen each other last, and he was finding it hard to act as if everything were normal.

"Sam, are you listening to anything I'm saying?"

"Oh, sorry. What?"

Mary laughed. "Do you get told off for not paying attention in school?"

"You've got no idea," Sam muttered to himself.

"I was saying that I found a book on Akhenaten. It might aid you on your water park quest." She slid a palm-sized book out of her handbag. "Don't worry— it's not very big. You won't get bogged down in any actual work. I even underlined some of the main points for you."

"Thanks."

Mary frowned. "Are you okay? You don't seem yourself. Well, what I mean is, you don't seem like the Sam I met yesterday."

For an awful moment Sam felt like he was about to start crying. He dropped his head as if his cup of orange juice suddenly needed his full attention. *No way. I am not going to start bawling in front of a girl I hardly know*, he thought as he scrambled to control himself.

"Sam, what's wrong?" There was real concern in Mary's voice now.

He took a few deep breaths, and when he was sure the danger had passed, he started talking.

SAM TOLD MARY THE WHOLE STORY. FROM the moment he got off the plane to meeting her at McDonald's. Afterward, he realized he'd been nervous about how she'd react—that she might tell him to stop acting so stupid and hand himself in to the police. But things didn't play out that way at all. The first thing she did was ask if he thought his uncle might have taken the money.

"No way," Sam insisted. "It's just not the kind of thing he would do. If you knew him, you'd know how crazy the idea was."

As Sam spoke, Mary nodded slowly, as though she

were a doctor consulting with a patient. Then she looked Sam in the eyes and promised to do everything she could to help. It felt weird . . . a good weird. Sam wasn't used to opening up to people. His school counselor would vouch for that. He had known Mary less than twenty-four hours, but he felt comfortable enough to admit how freaked out he'd been when the intruder had broken into the apartment. At that moment Sam was grateful to have Mary in his corner.

"If your uncle didn't steal the money, perhaps someone is trying to set him up. Can you think of any reason why?"

Sam chewed on his lower lip. "Maybe it's got something to do with this Akhenaten project."

"What about the metal detector?"

"He probably did take one of those. But he's allowed to. At the EEF they use them for their work."

The two clues Sam had found were on the table. Mary picked up the one that had been in the envelope. "Well, I can help you with this, for a start," she said.

Sam smiled. "I was hoping you could."

"Panehesy was one of Akhenaten's high priests. He's in that book I just gave you."

"What about those squiggly lines beside the name?"

"Some kind of hieroglyphics, but I'm not sure. As for this"—she pointed to the four triangles—"I have no idea what they mean. When was the last time you heard from your uncle?"

"His e-mail from Alexandria."

"Do you know exactly where he was in Alexandria?"

Sam shook his head. "All I know is he was doing some research on Akhenaten."

"And Panehesy," Mary added. "And if that piece of paper was worth hiding under his bed, it has to mean something." Mary took another sip of her chocolate milk. "That swipe card for your uncle's office. That will get you in?"

Sam thought back to his last visit to the Egyptian Exploratory Fund. Their budget didn't stretch far enough to cover flashy headquarters: Their office was on the fifth floor of a shabby old building not far from the McDonald's. From what Sam could remember, the swipe card got you in the front door of the building and into the office.

"It'll get me in," he said more confidently than he felt. "Why?"

"Well, I know a bit about computers. Your uncle's e-mail came from Alexandria, but it had to come through his company's server. If I had his server ID, I could probably find out exactly where your uncle was when he sent you that last e-mail."

"Okay." Sam had no idea what Mary was talking

about. "So, how do you find out what his server ID is?"

"I need you to send me an e-mail from his computer."

"You what?" Sam said. "I can't just go into my uncle's office and ask to use his computer. As soon as they see me, they'll call the cops."

"I know. You'll need to sneak in at night."

Sam searched Mary's face for a sign she was joking. "You want me to break into the EEF?"

Mary offered a weak smile. "It's not breaking in if you have a card. It's more like sneaking in. But you're right. You can't go in there while there are people around, can you? In fact, you probably shouldn't even be out at all. The police could be out looking for you right now."

Sam glanced around the room. It suddenly felt like everyone in the place was watching him.

"Relax," said Mary. "I've been keeping an eye out. No one's noticed you."

Two things occurred to Sam: The first was that he was going to have to start acting a lot smarter, or he wouldn't get far at all. *Of course* the cops could be out looking for him, and he just came wandering down to meet Mary like a stupid kid. The other thing that struck him was how composed Mary seemed about the whole situation.

"Have you done this kind of stuff before?"

"What? Help a friend, who I just met on a plane, find his missing uncle and at the same time avoid the local police? Of course," Mary said sarcastically. "I do it all the time."

Sam laughed. "It's just you seem kind of . . . I don't know. Like you know what you're doing."

"Well, it's a bit like Egyptology, isn't it?"

"Come again?"

Mary pointed at the pieces of paper on the table. "We follow the clues. Put the missing pieces together. And solve the problem, which in this case is finding your uncle."

Sam wasn't totally convinced by Mary's IKEA kitset take on his problem, but her attitude made him feel better, so he went with it. "Well, I guess I need to wait till tonight and then get into Jasper's office and on to his computer," he said with as much casual bravado as he could manage.

"Exactly. When you get there, send me an e-mail, and I'll take care of the rest. Have you got a mobile?"

Sam shook his head. In response, Mary slid a slim silver phone across the table. "You can borrow this. My number is already in it."

"Um, thanks."

"Don't mention it. So, what will you do now?"

"Head back to my uncle's, I guess."

"Aren't you afraid that whoever broke in might come back?"

This was something Sam had thought about. "My uncle rents a small storeroom down the hall from his apartment. There should be enough room for me. I could go there."

Mary nodded, and Sam was pleased to have been able to show he wasn't a complete amateur.

"Why don't you put this on," she said, taking a green army-style cap out of her bag. "It's not much of a disguise, but it will cover your face a bit."

"Wow, you really have thought about this, haven't you?"

"It's fun . . ." Mary stopped herself and looked nervously at Sam. "I'm sorry. I don't want you to think I am treating this like a joke. I'm not. Your uncle is missing. It must be terrible for you."

"That's okay," he said, trying to keep his voice level. "I'm grateful for the help."

Mary studied him. "There's no one you can call at home?"

"Back at school? No."

"Family?"

Sam's gaze reverted to his orange juice. "No, my uncle is my only family."

This was territory he didn't want to get into. Not even with Mary.

"We'll find your uncle. I promise."

Sam nodded, keeping his eyes on his glass.

"Well, at least you'll have something to read while you're holed up in your uncle's storeroom," Mary said, trying to lighten the atmosphere.

Sam picked up the Akhenaten book. Normally, something like this would be the last thing he'd consider opening, but everything had changed. This wasn't homework, it was a matter of life and . . . He refused to even think about the D-word. His uncle would be okay. He had to believe that. Sam was going to find him.

They were saying their good-byes on the footpath outside when Bassem pulled up in a shiny black SUV. Sam turned down Mary's offer of a ride back to his uncle's building, but as she climbed into the vehicle, he fought the urge to run after her. The SUV roared away from the curb and was soon lost in the sea of traffic. Feeling even more alone than before, Sam pulled his new hat down over his face like a celebrity trying to avoid the paparazzi and set off for his storeroom hideout.

Despite the new worry of being spotted by the police, Sam took the long way back to his uncle's building. He wasn't looking forward to being stuck in a small room for the rest of the day, and it was late morning by the time he got to Mitre Tower.

As well as Mary's book, Sam had one other piece of reading material to take to his hideout.

The envelope was sticking out of his uncle's mailbox when he entered the building. He recognized the logo of St. Albans School for Boys. He knew he had no place opening something addressed to Jasper, but it was going to concern him in some way and, given the circumstances, he decided it would be okay.

"Storeroom" was an exaggeration. "Store closet" was a more fitting description, Sam thought as he climbed over a broken coffee table and sat down on a folded rug. Luckily, there was a light, and the naked bulb gave the small space a soft yellow glow. Thin wooden shelves lined the walls from floor to ceiling, but they were empty except for a few old appliances and some plates and glasses. Sam put his sketch pad and book on the shelf next to him and made himself comfortable. Then he turned his attention to the letter.

As Sam suspected, the letter was an update on his counseling, but it didn't contain much he hadn't been told to his face. *Progress is slow but steady,* blah blah. *Sam still shows a reticence to really open up about the tragic events of his past,* blah blah.

Tragic events of his past.

It was such a nice, tidy way to sum it up. Sum up the moment Sam's life changed forever. His parents had both been Egyptologists with the EEF, like Jasper. After Sam's birth, his mother had stayed home in Boston with him, but they made regular trips to visit Sam's father on digs in Egypt. Five years ago his father left his job, and his parents took a romantic vacation in Jamaica, leaving Sam with his uncle in Cairo. The tragic event was their murder in a hotel room robbery. Overnight, Sam's idyllic life was obliterated. He was packed off to boarding school and allowed out only a couple of times a year to return to his uncle in Cairo.

He knew Uncle Jasper wasn't equipped to care for him twenty-four/seven, and he knew a dig site in the Egyptian desert wasn't the kind of place for a kid to grow up. But still . . . some part of him wished Jasper would've been more of a father figure.

St. Albans was a great school. It just wasn't . . . a *home*. Not like he'd grown up in.

His memories of Egypt before his parents' death were vague and muddled, but that particular trip wasn't. The day he was told the news—that exact moment when his uncle had sat him down on the sofa—was burned into his brain. Cairo was the place he'd been when his world had come crashing down, and it had always tainted his feelings about the city. What you love can be taken away in an instant, and there's nothing you can do about it. This was the driving force behind Sam's need to always be in control. At least that's what the counselor had told him.

The last part of the letter was about an increase in school fees and said information had been sent to the Verulam Corporation. The name was new to Sam. He'd always assumed his schooling was paid by his parents' estate.

Sam slid the letter back into its envelope and put it on a shelf behind him. Nothing in its pages could help him find his uncle, so he turned to the reading material Mary had given him, trying to ignore the lump in his throat. He would find Jasper. He *had to*. Sam wasn't sure what happened to thirteen-year-old boys with no family left, and he didn't want to find out.

Mary's words came back to him: *"We follow the clues. Put the missing pieces together. And solve the problem."* Sam wasn't sure if the book on Akhenaten would contain any important clues, but it would help take his mind off the task he faced that night.

5

THE MOLE

MORE THAN EIGHTEEN MILLION PEOPLE lived in Cairo, and on the streets that night Sam couldn't help but think that none of them liked to go home. The roads were tightly packed with horn-happy drivers, and the footpaths were overflowing as he made his way back downtown toward his uncle's office building.

Sam had spent the day reading and drawing. Not hugely different from a weekend back at boarding school. Those students who didn't go home on weekends were kept on a tight leash at St. Albans. Sam rowed on Saturdays; sports were compulsory, so he had picked the one that got him off the school grounds. The rest of the weekend was filled up with drawing and playing PlayStation with his roommates. He had been drawing a lot of zombies and hot rods lately. They were popular with the other boarders, which meant he could trade them for chocolate and other candy that was banned from the dorms. Normally, Sam could draw for hours, but stuck in the storeroom, with the evening's outing on his mind, he had found it hard to concentrate.

In the end, he decided to walk. Catching a taxi to the EEF offices would have made a dent in the limited funds he had left, and walking gave him a reason to get out of the apartment building earlier. His rowing coach would have been shocked to hear him admit it, but it felt good to get his legs moving. The one-hour trek also gave him time to get his head around what he was about to do.

Sam knew the way. He'd made the journey between the apartment and his uncle's office plenty of times, since Jasper didn't own a car. Sam wasn't even sure Jasper knew how to drive. Last summer Jasper had even let Sam walk the route by himself. It had happened only once, when his uncle had gone into work early, and Sam had been allowed to sleep in and walk to the EEF alone. Now, as he passed familiar landmarks, Sam remembered the excitement he'd felt that morning. He latched on to the memory, desperate to strengthen his resolve. But it soon faded into the night, leaving Sam with the reality of his plan.

It had already been a vacation of firsts. First police interview, first escape from the police, and now he was going to attempt his first break-in. Well, not a break-in in the strictest sense. He had a security card. But that didn't ease the sense of dread that hung over him.

Maybe I should just go to the police?

The thought kept popping into Sam's head, and the closer he got to his destination, the more appealing the idea was. But he knew how that would end. Him on a plane out of the country, his uncle lost forever or stuck in jail.

And he couldn't let that happen.

SAM STEPPED INTO THE DARKENED DOOR-way of a shop opposite the drab little building that housed the EEF. A single light lit the empty lobby area. The only activity in the building seemed to be on the eighth floor, which was the top one. Up there, Sam could see a few people moving from desk to desk. The rest of the building, including the EEF's office on the fifth floor, was in darkness.

Minutes ticked by. Sam told himself he needed to

wait, survey the scene, and make sure it was safe, but the truth was he was scared stiff and just putting off what came next. In the end it was the first signs of cramping that forced him into action. He thrust his hands into his pockets and stepped out onto the road. The high-pitched blast of an electric horn shattered the stillness of the empty street. Sam spun around and just missed being head butted by a screaming Egyptian wearing a motorbike helmet. Man and machine swerved wildly. Sam fell back onto the footpath, hitting his head on a steel garbage can. A hundred tiny stars swamped his vision, but through the haze he made out the motor-bike racing up the street, the rider still angrily shaking one arm.

Sam lay there, dazed and confused. Glancing over his shoulder he saw the alleyway that the speeding biker had popped out of. The far end of it was bathed in red light coming from a neon sign that proudly pro-claimed PIZZA ON WHEELS.

Calm had returned to the street, and Sam was just about to get to his feet when, out of the corner of his eye, he saw movement in the building. The lobby hadn't been empty after all. A security guard had been sitting out of sight behind the high reception desk. The incident in the street had stirred him into action.

Sam was still sprawled in front of the garbage can,

but there was no time to hide. Any movement now would draw the guard's attention, so he stayed exactly where he was. His only hope was that the shadows cast by the pizza shop would conceal him. That plan was shattered seconds later when the guard switched on the lobby lights, flooding the street in a golden glow.

Sam's cover was blown, his mission over before it had even started.

The guard moved to the doors and pressed his face against the glass. He was looking directly across the road. Sam could only watch and wait for a look of surprise to form on his face when he spotted a boy who seemed to be using a rubbish bin as a pillow.

But it didn't happen. Instead, the guard turned away, killed the lights, and walked out of sight. Lying there on the footpath, the only explanation Sam could think of was that the glare of the lights had worked in his favor, blinding the guard like a performer on a stage.

Disaster averted.

Sam got up and dusted himself off, but the problem of the guard still remained. Even with a swipe card, an American boy turning up in the middle of the night to access the EEF offices would seem odd.

Sam needed a way to get past the guard without being seen.

The light coming from the eighth floor revealed

perfectly smooth sides to the building. No way of climbing it. Anyway, who was he trying to kid? He wasn't Spider-Man. There was only one way in: through the front door.

So is that it? Sam wondered as he stood in the shop doorway. Had he failed before he had even begun? So far, all he had managed to accomplish was not getting run over by a pizza delivery guy.

The smell of freshly baked pizza wafted down the alleyway, teasing Sam's nose and reminding his stomach that it hadn't been fed since morning. Pizza was all Sam could think about, so he slipped around the corner and down the alleyway.

WITH HIS HANDS FULL, SAM WAS FORCED to kick the big door. The huge panels rattled horribly, and the guard leapt out of his seat. The glow from a small portable TV lit the scowl on his face as he left his desk.

"What do you want?" the man demanded.

"Delivery for the eighth floor," Sam mumbled from behind the stack of pizza boxes.

"I can see that," said the guard, "but there are no deliveries after nine thirty. They know that upstairs."

Sam kept his head down, hoping the cardboard wall and motorbike helmet would obscure his face. A glimpse of white skin would be sure to blow his cover.

The guard went silent, eyeing the pizza box tower through the glass. Sam wanted to plead his case, but was worried his dodgy Egyptian accent would give him away, so he remained silent. The standoff dragged on. Sam was on the verge of chickening out and making a run for it when he heard a *thunk* and felt a rush of chilled air spill from between the opening glass doors.

Sam mumbled a thank-you as he shuffled toward the elevators, but the guard didn't hear it. He'd already raced back to his desk, deciding that his TV show was more important than telling off a pizza delivery kid. He didn't bother to look up as the elevator doors opened. If he had, he would have been impressed with how easily the delivery boy managed to balance the huge stack of pizza boxes on one arm as he hit the eighth-floor button.

Not quite so impressive if you knew that all the boxes were empty.

THE ELEVATOR CREAKED AND GROANED in that alarming way that elevators in old buildings seem to do. Under normal circumstances that might have concerned Sam, but tonight it was the least of his worries.

It was thanks to Pizza on Wheels's recycling program that he'd been able to assemble his pizza wall. The helmet, which had also been in the Dumpster, was a bonus. If the security guard had taken a closer look, he would have noticed a huge chunk missing out of the back of it.

The creaking and groaning reached its climax as the elevator hit the eighth floor. It was a calculated risk, going to the only place in the building where there were people, but if the guard noticed the elevator stopping on the fifth floor, that would have been a bigger problem.

The *ping* that signaled the end of the journey was disturbingly loud. Sam stepped into a dimly lit hallway lined with doors. He turned from left to right, expecting one of the doors to burst open. Instead, the elevator shut and Sam was alone. Through the frosted glass panel in the door at the far end of the corridor he could see shapes of people moving about. He hurried in the opposite direction, through the door that led into a musty-smelling stairwell. As soon as he was through, Sam dumped the pizza boxes and helmet and raced down the stairs. The fifth-floor hallway was identical to the one on the eighth, but darker. There was no light coming from the door at the far end. Behind it were the empty offices of the EEF.

Sam moved fast. He was on the clock. Ten minutes, he figured, until the security guard started wondering why the pizza boy hadn't come back. Then a call would be made to the eighth floor. From what he'd seen, Sam didn't imagine the guard would actually get off his butt and go himself. But once the call went through, the pizza would hit the fan.

The small box next to the door beeped cheerfully when Sam swiped the security card across it. He slipped in and shut the door. It was a simple office. "Simple" had been Uncle Jasper's word. Sam's was "boring." Eight desks, set out in two rows of four, faced the windows. Apart from the large photos of famous Egyptian archaeological sites on the walls, a visitor might have thought it was an accountant's office. But now, in the darkness, with only the blue glow of sleeping computers to light the place, it looked much cooler. It felt like a scene from a science fiction movie, and Sam thought that was a vast improvement.

Jasper's desk was in the far corner, next to the window. As soon as Sam saw it, he knew something wasn't right. It was way too tidy. Sam's uncle treated his workspace like his apartment: a dump. Normally, there were piles of papers, stacks of books, and artifacts from Jasper's latest dig. Now it looked like an office desk in a catalog. A stapler and pen cup were lined up neatly behind a large desk pad next to Jasper's old computer.

Sam hit the power button, and while he waited for

the aging gray machine to come to life, he gave the desk a going-over and found nothing. The drawers were full of rubber bands, paper clips, and other assorted bits of stationery, but nothing more. If there had been any clues lying around, the person who had spring-cleaned Jasper's desk had taken them.

Valuable seconds ticked by, but finally the screen flashed into action. Sam's eyes had gotten used to the darkness, and it took a few moments to adjust to the harsh glare that came from the computer. He scanned the desktop for the small envelope icon and clicked on it. It was empty. The in-box, outbox, even the trash.

Had Jasper deleted it all to cover his tracks? Or did someone else do it for him?

Sam opened a new message, typed in the address he'd memorized, hit send, and then as the small arrow on the screen went around in circles, he took the mobile phone out of his pocket and hit the green button.

"Finally. I was starting to get worried," said Mary a few moments later. "What took so long?"

"I stopped for pizza."

"You what?"

"Nothing. Tell you later. You get the e-mail yet? I'm kind of in a hurry."

Mary laughed. "Well, soooorry. Got somewhere else to break into tonight?"

There was the tapping of keys over the phone, and then Mary spoke again. "Got it. Okay. I'm sending it straight back with an attachment. That's something you add—"

"I'm not completely computer illiterate. I just don't spend hours in front of them."

"Oh. Soooorry again."

A cartoon trumpet blast announced Mary's incoming message. Sam jumped, glancing behind him to be sure he was still alone. "I just got an e-mail from QZone73. That you?" Sam asked in a tone that sounded more relaxed than he really was.

"Kind of. It's an untraceable address. Now, listen, there should be a red box in it. That's the attachment."

Sam spotted a small red icon named Disc Candy. "I see it."

"You need to drag that onto the desktop and open it."

Sam did as he was told and the words CLICK TO ACCEPT popped up.

"Click," said Mary before Sam had a chance to speak.

Nothing happened.

"Now what?" asked Sam.

"Now we have to wait for a bit."

The question Sam desperately wanted to ask next was *How long?* He was getting cold and nervous. To take his mind off things, he picked up a pencil. He didn't bother fishing his sketchbook out of his pocket; the large, clean desk pad was begging to be used. Pepperoni pizza with extra cheese was the first thing that popped into Sam's head, so he went to work. "What's Disc Candy?" he asked as he drew.

"It's a mail mole."

"What does it do?"

"Well, it's complicated, but basically it's a program that will dig into the main server and tell us where your uncle was when he e-mailed you."

"Oh, *dig*. That's the mole part." Sam began applying the extra cheese to his pencil pizza. "So how do you know about this computery stuff?"

"Spoils of a misspent youth."

Sam stopped drawing. "What does that mean?"

There was another laugh on the other end of the line. "I'm not sure. I heard my father say it once. He's the one who taught me about computers. He's a bit of a whiz on them, and I guess I've picked up a few things over the years."

"I thought he was into Egyptology?"

"That's a hobby. Computers are his day job. That's how he made his millions."

It was Sam's turn to laugh. "Millions, eh? Now I don't feel so bad about you paying for my breakfast this morning."

Before Mary could reply, a small THANK YOU box appeared on the screen in front of Sam. "It's finished. Now what?"

"Well, it will take a while to do its thing. . . ."

Sam cut her off. "A while? Listen, I can't hang around here. I'm already pushing it as it is."

"That's cool. You don't need to stay. I can monitor the mole from here."

"Oh, okay. All right, then." Sam wondered if Mary had detected the trace of panic in his voice. If she did, she didn't let on. "Do I need to leave the computer on? Someone could notice."

"Nope. It's doing its magic in the server, not the computer. I'll ring you as soon as I know anything. What will you do now?"

Sam realized he hadn't thought that far ahead. "Probably go back to Jasper's storeroom. Keep out of sight."

"Okay. Well, I'll ring as soon as I have anything, I promise. You take care."

"No worries," Sam said lightly, overdoing the cheerfulness to make up for the previous outburst.

Sam put the phone back in his pocket and switched the computer back to sleep mode. The blue glow that spilled across the desk pad added a trippy sci-fi look to his pizza sketch.

He was about to stand up when he noticed something odd. There were *letters* on his pepperoni pizza. He hadn't drawn them. They had appeared when he had been adding the extra cheese. The shading had revealed grooves in the paper made when someone, presumably his uncle, had written on the sheet that had once been on top.

Sam remembered seeing a detective movie where they had done the same thing on a pad next to a telephone to find a number, and it gave him an idea. He began gently shading the area around the sketch. Other letters quickly appeared and finally two numbers.

The day before, it would have meant nothing to Sam, but the reading up on Akhenaten had paid off. Nefertiti, he now knew, was Akhenaten's queen. He wasn't sure about the 18. Maybe it was her age. Now he had something else to add to his growing collection of confusing clues.

Sam quickly removed the top page of the desk pad and then ran for the door. His time was well and truly up. He could only hope that the guard was so caught up in his TV show that the pizza boy had slipped his mind.

Sacrificing silence for speed, Sam tore down the five sets of stairs like it was an Olympic sport, pausing only when he reached the fire exit on the ground floor. This was the moment of truth. If the guard or, even worse, the police, was looking for him, they would surely have posted someone on the exit. There were two options: open the door as silently as possible and check the coast was clear, or go for it.

In the end Sam opted for a mix of the two. As quietly as he could, he unhooked the locking bar so the door would swing free. Then he took a deep breath and booted it open.

He went left, because that was the way the door opened. As he sprinted along the back alley, he waited for startled cries to break out behind him, but the only noise he heard was the thumping of feet on the concrete. His feet. He made it to the corner of the building, and a quick look behind told him what he had already worked out—the alley was empty.

Keeping to the shadows Sam moved down the side of the building, back toward the street. The danger was over. The tension that had built up in him over the past few hours melted away. He'd made it in and out of the EEF office, in the middle of the night, without getting caught.

Back at St. Albans, Sam and his roommates had come up with a dare called The Mission. It involved sneaking out of the school at night to buy junk food at the local 7-Eleven. In theory it was totally doable. The boys had the route planned out. Sam had even sketched it. Out of the second-story window, down the drainpipe, across the lawn, and over the wall. From the safety of their beds at night there was always plenty of big talk, but no one had ever done it. Sam had gotten closest. One night he'd made it as far as the drainpipe before getting cold feet.

Now, walking down one of Cairo's back streets, Sam wondered how the 7-Eleven thing had ever been a big deal. He was buzzing. He wanted to ring his roommates and impress them with his exploits. He wondered if the phone Mary had given him would make international calls.

By the time he had reached the main road, Sam had calmed down, and his thoughts drifted back to pizza. But for much more obvious reasons this time. He was starving.

6

END OF THE
NIGHT SHIFT

SAM WAS ON HIS THIRD SLICE OF A
pepperoni pizza that tasted only slightly better than
his drawing would have. It had taken another chunk
out of his cash reserves, but what bothered him was the
feeling he wasn't any closer to finding his uncle, despite
the risks he'd taken. Sam had been sure he would find
a solid lead at his uncle's desk. Instead, he'd ended up
with another cryptic clue. He hoped Mary's e-mail hunt
would uncover something.

The thrill of getting away with the break-in had
faded, and in its place came tiredness. Sitting at the
chipped Formica table in the harshly lit twenty-four-hour

snack food joint, his task seemed impossible. This was the state he was in when Mary called, which made it even harder to decipher the flurry of words that poured out of the phone.

"Sam, you were right! Your uncle is in trouble; he's been set up. He tried to e-mail you, but you didn't get it!"

Sam struggled to keep up with what Mary was telling him. "An e-mail? What does it say?"

There was a brief silence on the other end, and when Mary spoke again she'd calmed down a fraction. "The mole found an e-mail sent by your uncle last Thursday morning at one a.m."

"From Alexandria?"

"No. He sent it from the EEF office. He must have come back to Cairo."

"But I never got it."

"I know!" Mary struggled to contain her excitement. "Someone intercepted the message."

"Why would they do that?"

"To keep you from reading it? Make sure you came to Cairo? Maybe they wanted you to lead them to your uncle. Look, the mole is still tracking the location of the Alexandria e-mail, but I'm going to send you this new one now, so you can read it for yourself. But don't you see, Sam? You were right about your uncle."

The wannabe pizza sat forgotten on the plate. Sam stared at his cell phone. The seconds passed like minutes until the small envelope icon flashed up. Sam clicked and read the message his uncle had wanted him to get three days earlier.

From: Jasper Force j.force@eef.com

Date: Thursday, July 23, 2015 at 01:07 AM

To: s.force@stalbans.com

My Sam,

Things have taken an unexpected turn in the past few days. I have just found out I am about to be accused of stealing a large amount of money from my employers. I won't go into all the details, but needless to say the allegations are completely false. I fear this setup is to do with my recent trip to Alexandria.

I'm afraid I can't say any more than that now. At this stage I am not sure whom to trust. I've come into the office like a thief in the night, but all I'll be leaving with is one of the metal detectors.

The other reason for my nocturnal visit was to send you this e-mail. I don't think it's safe for you to visit right now. Can you please arrange to stay over at St. Albans for the next week?

I'm leaving Cairo now and intend to continue my original research, which I will follow to the source. I am not sure how long it will be before I can get in touch again. I have reason to believe I'm being followed, so I think it prudent to keep you out of it.

I know this must all sound a bit dramatic from where you are sitting in Boston, and it could well turn out to be the overfired imagination of a silly old man, but better to be safe than sorry, eh?

Sit tight, my boy. I will be in touch soon. I promise.

xxx Jasper

The e-mail recharged Sam's batteries. He read and reread it half a dozen times. There was no sign of a hidden message in this one, but his uncle had made his intentions clear. The "original research" he referred to had to be Akhenaten, and following it "to the source" could mean only one place: the city Akhenaten built as his new capital, El Amarna. Thanks to the map in Mary's book, he knew exactly where that was.

Sam checked his watch and was amazed to see it was three a.m. He still had a long walk back to the apartment, but that was nothing compared to the nearly two hundred miles he would have to cover to get to the city Akhenaten built to worship the sun god Aten. For that trip Sam was going to need more cash.

It was nearly sunrise by the time he got back to Mitre Tower, but the walk had only fired Sam up even more. Questions and plans—and more plans and more questions—were bouncing around in his head. He didn't know exactly where his uncle was in Amarna, but maybe the note he'd found on the desk pad was related to that. He decided to tackle one problem at a time. First, he needed cash, then transport to Akhenaten's city.

The plan was to get some sleep in the storeroom, scour the apartment for money, and then hit the road. But standing there in the hallway Sam changed his mind. He wasn't going to be able to sleep. Why try? Better to keep moving.

Before he entered the apartment, Sam listened for signs there was someone inside. When he didn't hear anything, he unlocked the door. Everything was just as he'd left it. The question on his mind was whether Jasper had left any money. Sam vaguely remembered a small tin Jasper used to fish cash out of before they went out. A brown tin with a red lid. The kind you see in the kitchen. Sam started there. After all, he knew Jasper didn't come up with the most original hiding places.

Sure enough, in the cupboard above the sink was a tidy row of small brown tins with red lids. Each one was labeled. There was salt, pepper, curry. . . . He never got any further, because an arm inside a thick woolen sweater snaked itself around his chest and wrenched him away from the sink. Sam cried out in surprise as he was pulled back against the body of a large man.

"Sam, listen to me. I have to talk to you." The voice sounded muffled and terrifying. Sam was listening, all right, but he'd heard enough.

Pure terror drove him now. The man's grip was strong, and Sam felt like he was caught in a giant padded vise. What came next wasn't based on anything he'd been taught or seen. It was purely instinct. There was no way he could break his captor's grip. Especially being held from behind. So, instead, he dropped. Straight down to the floor.

The move caught the man by surprise. One second he had the kid in a bear hug. The next he was hugging air. Sam hit the deck on all fours, scuttled toward the door, then sprang to his feet and ran like hell. He shot out of the apartment like a human cannonball, smashing into the wall opposite before regaining his balance and tearing off down the hall.

The heavy thumping of boots told him what was happening behind. Then the man's voice echoed down the corridor, angrier, more urgent. "Sam, wait! . . . outside!"

The man's pleas fell on deaf ears. Deaf ears attached to a fast-moving boy. Sam's only thought was he had to get to the stairs at the other end of the corridor as rapidly as possible.

Up ahead a shaft of light lit up the floor, and, just like that, a new escape route presented itself. One of the elevators had opened, and a weary night-shift worker in blue overalls stepped out, right into the oncoming traffic. Sam grabbed him by the arm. It was the only way to stop himself. His momentum spun him around the stunned man and catapulted him into the empty elevator. He lunged for the small button at the bottom of the panel. The one with two arrows pointing together. As the steel doors began their agonizingly slow slide together, Sam got his first glimpse of his attacker. A big, black mass. Black coat, black baseball cap pulled down over a bushy black beard. He had also built up considerable speed coming down the hall, but his stop was far less graceful than Sam's. He plowed right into the dazed victim, and the last thing Sam saw was a tangled mess of blue and black arms. Then the doors finally met in the middle.

Instead of the gentle vibration as the elevator began its journey, the small space shook violently as meaty fists pounded on the doors. Something was wrong, but in his panicked state Sam couldn't work out why the elevator wasn't moving. The banging stopped, and two rows of pink fingertips sprouted in the crack between the doors.

The man was trying to pry the elevator open.

Sam was seconds from being caught, and then the answer hit him. In his panic to get the doors closed, he'd forgotten what came next. He thumped the G button repeatedly. At first the elevator refused to respond, and then finally the steel box gave a short shudder, the fingers retracted, and Sam was lowered out of danger.

The only thing that had saved him, he realized, was the fact that in his own haste the man chasing him had forgotten to push the elevator call button. That would have opened the doors instantly and sealed Sam's fate.

Gasping for breath Sam watched the small glowing lights above the door count off the floors. He was sure the man couldn't make it down seventeen flights of stairs as fast as the elevator, but what if another elevator had been waiting?

Eight . . . seven . . . six . . . Sam rocked nervously. What next? The doors would open soon. What should he do then?

In the end, his legs did the thinking. The elevator stopped, and before the doors were halfway open, Sam had squeezed through and bolted. As he ran across the foyer, he played back the scene in the hallway. The man had been shouting something about "downstairs." But it was all a blur, and the only thing he could focus on was the need to get away from the man upstairs.

Sam burst out through the front doors of Mitre Tower, sending them flying back on their hinges and smashing into their respective doorstops. The double whammy created a noise that echoed up and down the street. It took a few more moments for Sam to realize it had been a fatal mistake.

The noise would have woken the dead. It definitely

woke the man sleeping in the car across the road. As Sam ran onto the street, he saw the man wake with a start and turn toward the building to identify the source of the noise. His eyes locked onto Sam. There was a flash of recognition, and then he started to get out of the car.

"There's someone downstairs." The words the bearded man had been yelling assembled themselves in the correct order in Sam's memory. The sight of this new threat drove Sam on, and he sprinted past the car and into the darkened alleyway that led to the maze.

7

MYSTERY SHOPPER

"SOUK" IS THE ARABIC NAME FOR THE
local market. There are all kinds of souks, named after
the products they specialize in, but the souk across the
road from Jasper's apartment sold all kinds of stuff. It
was a rabbit warren of narrow interconnected alleys,
lined with tiny shops offering everything from plastic
buckets to fake Rolexes. Sam's nickname for the place
was the Stuff Maze and he'd gotten lost in it more than
once. This time he wanted to lose the man chasing him.

A few hundred feet in and he was already hopelessly
disoriented, but what had become clear was that his
hope of losing himself in a sea of people was never

going to happen. Sam had never ventured into the souk this early in the morning. If he had, he would have known that it was a ghost town at this hour.

He took the first left, then a right. Then the alley forked, and he went right again. He couldn't hear if he was being chased and wasn't going to waste time checking behind him.

The alleyways were narrow and long. As he dodged the piles of fake plastic flowers and stacks of pots blocking his path, Sam knew his pursuer would be able to track him easily. He had to get off the street. At the next tiny intersection he went right, then quickly took another right and saw what he was looking for: an open door.

Food shop? Home goods? Clothing store? Sam had no idea. He spotted a bit of everything as he darted in, almost tripping over the low counter. A startled old man appeared from behind a newspaper. Sam smiled awkwardly and tried to look as if he knew what he'd come for.

Compared to some of the other stores in the souk, this one was reasonably large—almost the size of his uncle's apartment. There were three ceiling-high shelves running the length of the space, with just enough room at each end to get around. They were packed with pots, plastic bowls, and other shelf-sized household items. Sam hurried to the farthest corner from the door and proceeded to show a lot of interest in the goods displayed down at floor height. From his crouched position he was able to peer through the gaps in the three shelves and out the dirty window, into the alley.

He watched and waited.

The gentle rustle of newspaper told Sam that the shop owner hadn't moved from his seat behind the counter. Perhaps he was used to young western boys running into his shop first thing in the morning.

Seconds ticked by. Sam could hear two men talking farther down the alley, but apart from that, the place seemed deserted. Another rustle of the paper signaled the turning of a page. Perhaps the shopkeeper had forgotten about him? For the first time, Sam focused on the items on the shelf right in front of him. They were mostly schoolbooks. A quick scan of the rest of the shelves revealed nothing of interest, and Sam was about to go back to his peephole onto the alley when something made him take another look at the books. The one on the top of the pile was about the size of a notepad. The title read *Hieratic Numerals*, but it was the little scribbles underneath that had caught his eye. They looked exactly like the ones from the piece of paper under his uncle's bed. Before Sam had a chance to open the book, he heard someone else enter the shop.

"Excuse me," said a man with a thick European accent. "I'm looking for my son. He came this way, I think. Have you seen him?"

Sam froze. It had to be the man from the car. Suddenly, his hideout felt like a trap. Why had he taken the first open door he found?

There was more paper rustling, and then the man spoke again. "Have . . . you . . . seen . . . a boy? A . . . boyyyy?"

Sam had been thrown a lifeline: The shopkeeper didn't speak English.

"Forget about it," said the man in frustration. There were more footsteps. Was he leaving? Sam could only crouch there and hope, but then a high shrill filled the shop and ruined everything. The footsteps stopped as Sam fumbled for the ringing cell phone in his pocket, but it was too late. He was busted.

THERE WAS ONLY ONE WAY OUT OF THE shop, but Sam had two ways to get there. Back down the aisle and straight past the counter, or head to the front of the shop, then down to the door.

Two became one when the man appeared at the far end of the shelf. He was bigger than he'd seemed in the car. Or maybe it was the cramped space in the store. Sam had thought he was bald, but now he could see the man had blond hair, but shaved so short there was almost no trace of it. And then Sam noticed his boots. They were black and polished. The last time he'd seen them they had been inches from his face.

The Short-Haired Man wasn't moving. He didn't have to. Sam was trapped. Whichever way he tried to run, the man could easily move to block him.

"It seems you gave my colleague the slip, Sam." The man had a European accent. His tone was soft and patronizing. "Perhaps we should go now, yes?"

They were facing each other like gunfighters. Unarmed gunfighters. But then Sam realized he had plenty of ammo. Shelves full of it. Jars of olives were lined up at head height, so Sam grabbed one with each hand and hurled them down the aisle.

The Short-Haired Man laughed as the first one smashed near his boots. The startled cry from the counter told Sam that the shop owner had had a very different attitude. But the laughing stopped when the second bottle of olives exploded on the wall, showering Sam's target with olives and shards of glass. The color of his face changed to a mottled red. He bellowed in anger and charged down the aisle.

Sam had just made things much, much worse. He

stumbled back, and around the end of the shelf. The empty middle aisle lay in front of him. It seemed like the quickest way out, so he took it, but halfway down, he realized it was a big mistake.

Three bags of flour exploded off the shelf in front of him. An open hand followed and swung wildly at Sam, forcing him to stop dead in his tracks. Through a gap in the shelf he caught a glimpse of the Short-Haired Man, wide-eyed and angry. Another hand punched its way through. The aisle wasn't wide enough to step back. All Sam could do was duck under as the first hand swung past.

"Where you going, Sam?" the man taunted. "Left? Right?"

He had Sam trapped again, but this time only the shelf separated them. The man lunged through another gap, lower this time, and Sam didn't see the hand coming. There was a yell of triumph as Sam's leg was caught and pulled toward the shelf. His body hit the shelf so hard, the whole thing wobbled like a badly built fence, and at that moment Sam saw a way out. He placed both hands on the shelf above his head and pushed.

The next noise was one of surprise, followed quickly by a scream as the entire shelf unit toppled over.

The man let go of Sam and tried to get out of the

way, but gravity won. He'd moved only a couple of feet before the ceiling-high wall of goods crashed on top of him.

It wasn't fatal, not by a long shot. Sam could hear the man screaming and cursing. Behind the counter the shop owner was cowering under his newspaper.

"Sorry about that," Sam said as he ran out the door.

The incident in the shop hadn't gone unheard. People were popping out from behind every door, transforming the place into the souk Sam was more familiar with.

He fought the urge to run, and it paid off. Strolling casually down the alley, a young white boy was completely ignored by nosy neighbors eager to investigate the ruckus that had disturbed their morning.

Sam headed deeper into the souk. He may have been moving at the pace of a kid without a care in the world, but his mind was going a million miles an hour. The shop owner would get over his shock and was sure to get the police involved, and as if that weren't enough, there was still the problem of the Short-Haired Man and the stranger who'd staked out his uncle's apartment. Things were going from bad to worse. So far Sam had been lucky, but how long could his streak last? He had to get off the street. Fast.

The solution was waiting around the next corner.

Two words that told him this was the perfect place to lie low for a while: KEEP OUT.

8

A FAMILIAR FACE

"SORRY ABOUT BEFORE," MARY SAID WHEN
she answered the phone. "Did my call wake you up?"

Sam laughed. "Not exactly."

"So, what were you doing?"

"It's a long story. I'll tell you about it later. Listen, I think I worked out one of the clues."

"Well, I've got some news too. You go first."

"Okay. You know those squiggles beside the name Panehesy? They're Egyptian hieratic numerals."

There was a brief pause on the other end of the line. "How did you work that out?"

"I found a book in a shop."

"You went shopping?" Mary sounded surprised.

"Not by choice, believe me."

"So what do these hieratic numerals mean?"

"Well, that's the thing," said Sam, "I don't know yet. I had to leave the shop in a hurry and forgot the book. I was wondering if you could find some info on hieratic numbers and send it to me."

"No problem. But, Sam, you really shouldn't be wandering into shops in the daytime. There could be people looking for you!"

Mary didn't know the half of it.

"Anyway, here's my news. The mole tracked down the location of the computer your uncle e-mailed you from in Alexandria. I was worried it might be an Internet café or motel, but it's more interesting than that."

"Okay." Mary had Sam's complete attention.

"The Port Authority. They're responsible for all the ships that come in and out of Alexandria."

Sam didn't say anything.

"Are you still there?" asked Mary.

He was. He was just confused. "What does that mean? Why would he be at the Port Authority?"

"Well, I don't know exactly, but it must have something to do with why he was in trouble. Maybe he was expecting a shipment. Did he mention anything like that to you?"

"No. Nothing. He said he was doing research on Akhenaten."

Mary hurried on. "Look, it doesn't matter. We know he was there, and I know someone in Alexandria who will go to the office and find out why." She paused. "Well, Bassem does," she admitted.

"Bassem will do that for me?"

"No," said Mary. "But he'll do it for me."

Sam could tell by the way she'd replied that her answer was directed at two sets of ears. His and a pair that was in the room with her. "It will take a bit of time for our man in Alexandria to do his thing. What are you going to do until then?"

It was odd the way Mary referred to "our man in Alexandria," as though she were a spy chief or something, but Sam didn't say anything. He was getting the feeling there was more to Mary than met the eye. "I need to get to Amarna," he answered.

"Are you still in your uncle's storeroom? We could come and get you."

"I kind of had to leave there in a hurry. I'm in a new place."

"What? Where?"

"A shop."

"A shop? Is that safe?"

"This one is. It's empty," said Sam.

"Empty" was an understatement. "Completely gutted" was more accurate. A concrete shell with a boarded-up door and windows.

"How did you end up in an empty shop?" asked Mary.

"Well, like I said, it's a long story. I got back to the apartment building, but I wasn't tired, so . . ." Sam's recap of the morning's events came to halt. "Mary, I have to go."

"Why? Is something wrong?"

"No, no. Not really. I just saw someone I know."

"I thought I was the only person you knew in Cairo," Mary said almost indignantly.

"Look, there's no time to explain. I'll call you later." Sam felt bad hanging up on her, but he'd just spotted the only other person he could trust in Cairo, right outside his hideout.

"HADI! HADI! PSSST!"

Sam could tell Hadi had heard his name the first time, but it took him a couple of seconds to work out where the voice was coming from. Finally, Hadi turned to face the empty shop and met Sam's eyes through a gap in the boards covering the window.

"Sam Force? Is that you?"

Sam nodded.

"I've been looking for you, my friend."

"Looking for me? Why?"

Hadi glanced left and right, checking that it was safe to talk. Then he leaned closer to the window and lowered his voice. "Sam, my friend, you made big trouble in that shop this morning. Police, they are everywhere, and they all have photos of you. When I see the trouble you are in, I think maybe if I could find you, I can help. But you found me, yes? How can I help?"

Sam answered instantly. "I need to get to Amarna."

Hadi didn't reply, and instead he disappeared from Sam's sight. Sam worried he might have scared the taxi driver off with his request. "Hadi? Are you still there?"

"Yes, Sam. Amarna is far from Cairo."

"Two hundred miles. I have a map."

"A thing like this may take some time to arrange."

"And I don't have much money." Sam was worried that the confession could be a deal breaker, but Hadi was unfazed.

"No problem. I do this because you are my friend, yes?"

"Yes," answered Sam gratefully.

"For now, you wait here, yes?"

"Sure."

Sam heard the shuffle of feet on the pavement and knew Hadi had gone.

SAM RECEIVED TWO DELIVERIES THAT afternoon.

The first, from Mary, was a graph of Egyptian hieratic numerals. Sam laid the Panehesy note next to the picture he'd received in the text message and proceeded to decode the squiggles.

Egyptian Hieratic Numerals

1	*ı*	10	ᴧ	100	⌐	1000	⅃
2	*ıı*	20	⅄	200	⌐⌐	2000	⅃″
3	*ııı*	30	X	300	⌐ᵘ	3000	⅃‴
4	*ıııı*	40	⌐	400	⌐ᵘⁱ	4000	⅃⁗
5	7	50	₹	500	⌐‴	5000	⅃″ ⅃″
6	2	60	⅏	600	⌐‴	6000	⅀″
7	₹	70	⅄	700	⌐ɔ	7000	⅀ᵖ
8	₌	80	Щ	800	⌐ᵘ	8000	⅀‴
9	₹	90	⅏	900	⌐ᵉⁱ	9000	⅀‴

Panehesy ⟨ıı ⌐ 8″⌿⟩

One thousand nine hundred forty-two was the answer. But the answer to what?

The second delivery came in the more traditional form: a box.

A shoe box, to be specific.

A shoe box for a pair of size 10, brown suede business shoes, to be *really* specific.

The box came in the same way Sam had—through the small gap under the boards that were nailed across the doorway. He wasn't expecting to see a pair of size 10 brown suede business shoes when he removed the lid, but what he did find shocked him.

It looked like a handgun from the future. Sleek and black, with a small telescopic sight mounted on the top. Only the chunky silver lettering on the side ruined the look—SPACE RANGER LASER. Sam had no illusions about the weapon's laser capabilities, but he couldn't resist trying it out. Aiming across the room, he pulled the trigger. The tip of the barrel glowed bright green as a small pellet shot out. It hit the wall with a sharp *clack* and bounced back across the floor. With a newfound respect for his Space Ranger Laser, Sam placed it on the floor and continued going through the box.

The next item was a crudely drawn street map that began at a point S, which Sam guessed was the souk, and ended at somewhere called T 6. There was also a flashlight, a Snickers bar, and a necklace with a scarab beetle like the one Hadi had hanging in his taxi. Under all that was a note.

Sam put on the necklace and ripped open the Snickers. He hadn't eaten since the early morning pizza. His diet definitely wouldn't get the approval of the school nurse, but it was just what he needed. He devoured the bar as he read what Hadi had to say.

Sam,

It is better for me to give you your instructions like this. Police are still looking for you, my friend, I am told there is a reward for you now.

Do not worry. I know a man; his name is Kareem. He has a truck going to Al Minya. This is very close to Amarna. He will take you as favor for me. Be ready at 10.

I will make a distraction. When you hear it, leave the shop. Go left to the first alley, and there you will see the entrance to the sewer.

It is too dangerous for you to be on the streets, even at night. The sewer is better.

Follow my map. It will take you to the compound where Kareem's truck is. But

when you reach it WAIT INSIDE!
There are guards at the trucks.
Kareem will open the sewer at 6 sharp.
Be there, Sam. He will not wait.

Remember, you must follow the map
exactly: The sewer system is big—
maybe as big as Cairo itself. There are
not many ways out. If you get lost,
you will stay lost.

Your good friend,
Hadi

Now the rough map made sense and the hastily drawn lines looked more ominous. Not simple streets, but tunnels under the city. Stinky tunnels, Sam suspected. Still, it didn't sound like he had much choice. But why the toy gun?

He found out when he turned the piece of paper over.

The gun is good, yes? This is a gift,
from a shop owner who will not miss it.
Use it for protection. And the necklace
is my gift to you, Sam. Remember, it will
bring you luck. Make sure you put it on.

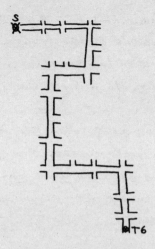

Sam was touched by the gift of the necklace, but was Hadi having a laugh about the gun? Protection from what? Space monsters?

FOR SAM, THE REST OF THE DAY DRAGGED on like math class. Complete and utter boredom, interrupted only by short periods of sleep. It wasn't that he found math or any of his other classes hard. He just couldn't see the point. Why study? Why go to all the effort if your life could be over just like that? Another symptom of someone who had suffered a huge personal tragedy? So Sam was told. But sometimes he wondered if it was just the way he was. After all, who really knew where the original Sam stopped and the Sam who had lost both parents started? He didn't. But he had learned how the game worked. He always did just enough schoolwork to avoid being called to the counselor for another chat.

Sam didn't call Mary back. He knew she'd ring him if she had news, but he was starting to have second thoughts. There was something too . . . *composed* about her. Like she did stuff like this every day. He couldn't help but be the tiniest bit suspicious. In the end, he did send her a text telling her his friend had arranged a ride to Amarna for him, but he left out most of the details, just in case.

Night fell and, like all cities across the Middle East, things got busier. People lived their life at the end of the day in this part of the world. As zero hour approached and the foot traffic increased, Sam tried to work out what Hadi had planned. What if he missed the signal? Or worse, what if Hadi's distraction wasn't distracting enough? If it drew more people near his hideout but didn't hold their attention, that would just make things worse. He could end up crawling straight into a trap.

He needn't have worried. When ten o'clock rolled around, Sam and everyone else in the souk heard Hadi.

9
THE TALKING BRIDGE

SAM DIDN'T SEE ANYTHING, BUT HE HEARD
it. A small motorbike, going too fast, crashed into a
wall, triggering a barrage of angry screams.

What happened next drew Sam to the window in
a hurry.

Another crashing sound, but this was like an old
wooden shed exploding. It was immediately followed by the distressed squawks of lots and lots of
chickens. Through the gaps in the boarded window,
it looked like a giant pillow fight had just taken
place. It was only when Sam spotted Hadi, standing
in the middle of the feathery crash site, wearing a

helmet, that Sam realized: This was the distraction.

Flimsy crates had burst apart, and the feathered prisoners, who all seemed to have escaped unharmed, were making an unorganized bid for freedom. The problem was, despite the spectacle, it didn't seem to have attracted much attention, and the doorway to the hideout was still dangerously exposed.

But Sam was about to find out that he didn't know the residents of the souk as well as Hadi did.

Within the next thirty seconds, the scene was flooded with open arms and hungry mouths as everyone within earshot came after a free meal. The noise made by the eager bargain hunters and their prey rose to rock-concert levels, and then the shrill pitch of a siren was thrown into the mix as a policeman on a motorbike rolled in. Sam was worried that this would spoil Hadi's plan, but instead of attempting to control the situation the policeman tore off his helmet and joined the chicken run.

The street was packed with people. It was time for Sam to leave.

His first attempt failed as a distraught hen charged in through the small gap at the bottom of the door, sending Sam back on his butt. The new tenant fled to the back of the empty shop, and Sam tried again.

He crawled out into the crowd and then, keeping

his head down, got to his feet and went left, looking for the alleyway.

The entrance to the sewer was right where Hadi said it would be. An empty Coke can jammed under the manhole cover made it easy for Sam to push it aside.

As he climbed down the narrow iron ladder, Hadi came running down the alley.

"Good, you found it," said the young taxi driver as he spat chicken feathers out of his mouth.

"Yeah, thanks. You come to see me off?"

"I'll put manhole cover back," Hadi replied, skidding to a stop. "Need to make sure you are not followed." He motioned back up the alley. "You like my distraction?"

Sam nodded. "Very original. Where'd you find so many chickens?"

"Ah." Hadi smiled. "I take a job this afternoon as chicken delivery boy." He nodded back toward the street, where the free food rumble raged on. "Job not work out so well. I might go back to taxi, eh?"

"Sure. But maybe you should keep the crash helmet." Hadi didn't get the joke, so Sam changed the subject. "Hey, thanks for all your help. I don't know how I can repay you for—"

Hadi cut him off. "Sam. I do this for you . . . as a friend. You have everything?"

"Yep." The flashlight was in his back pocket, and

Sam could feel the gun digging into the small of his back. "I've got everything."

"What about the necklace. You have it on, yes?"

"Yes," said Sam, tapping his chest. "It's right here."

Hadi knelt down. "Good. It brings much luck. You go now. But remember, you must be at the truck depot by six. If you are not, Kareem will go."

"Don't worry. I'll be there."

There was an awkward pause, with Sam on the ladder, only his head sticking out, and Hadi kneeling next to him. Sam wasn't sure what to say, but then it clicked that Hadi was waiting for him to go so he could close the manhole.

"Right, I'll be off, then."

"Good luck, Sam," Hadi called out as he slid the heavy steel lid back into position.

With a heavy *thunk*, Sam's world went black, but all he could think about were his parting words to Hadi: *"I'll be off, then."* He'd sounded like a lame character in a bad movie.

As he climbed down the ladder, Sam kicked himself for not thinking to take a look where he was headed when he had the chance. It was too risky to take the flashlight out of his pocket now, so he just kept climbing down. And down. And down. When his feet hit water, he figured he'd reached the bottom. When the water was up to his waist, he decided it was time for the flashlight.

The sewer was much bigger than Sam had expected. More like an underground canal. The beam from the flashlight only just reached the roof. Directly above him, Sam could just make out the hole the ladder came out of. It dropped straight down, but behind it, a few feet above the waterline, was a narrow path. When he'd read Hadi's sewer plan, Sam had naturally thought of the kind of sewage that got flushed down the toilet. It was a relief to discover he was standing in merely stagnant water—probably just storm water runoff.

He climbed back up to the path and checked the map and the time on his cell phone. It was ten thirty. Plenty of time to get to Kareem. Or so he thought.

IT TOOK THIRTY MINUTES TO GET TO THE first intersection. By then Sam had worked out that Cairo's old sewage system was a lot bigger than it looked on his badly drawn map. Now Hadi's insistence about being at the truck depot by six made more sense. Sam had a lot of ground to cover, and the condition of the path didn't help. It was covered in slime and crumbling away in some places, so he had to watch his step.

He picked up the pace and made better time to the second intersection. Like the first, there was a flimsy metal bridge across the intersecting waterway. He crossed straight over, but not because he was confident it was safe. Far from it. The thing looked like it had been made out of wire coat hangers assembled by blind men. But Sam had no choice. Using the bridge was much faster than wading through the water, and if it failed, that's where he'd end up anyway. The rusted metal joints screeched as he wobbled his way across. The same thing happened on the next bridge.

That was how he discovered that he was being followed.

At the third intersection he took the bridge that went right and into a new tunnel. He had just crossed and the sounds of the squeaking joints were still ringing in his ears. The noise continued for a few more moments before he realized it wasn't in his ears at all. The noise was coming from the bridge. Sam turned and shined the flashlight back at the bridge, but there was no one there. Then he lowered the beam of light down to the walkway to see it was alive with a tightly packed mass of wriggling brown and black bodies.

He was being followed by hundreds of giant rats.

They were covering every spare inch of the floorboards, and it was their collective weight that made the bridge wobble and gave away their position.

As the flashlight played across them, they froze.

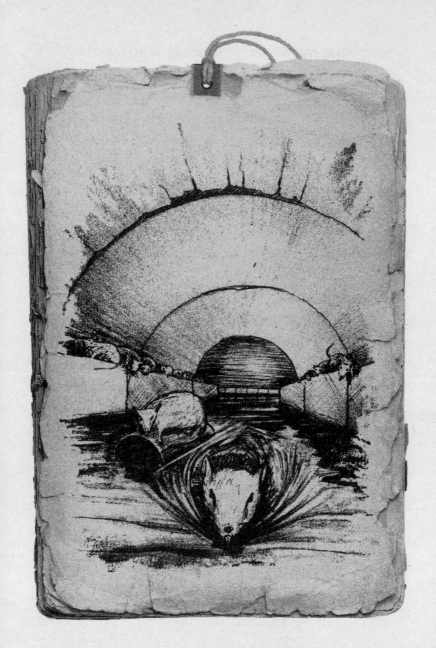

Hundreds of tiny black eyes locked on to Sam. He felt as if they were waiting for him to make his next move. Daring him to do something. So he did.

Raising the flashlight like a club, he lunged forward, screaming.

Nothing. The furry mob didn't flinch. All eyes remained on Sam, and it freaked him out. It was as if they were saying, *Is that the best you've got?*

It wasn't.

The green glow from the barrel of the Space Ranger Laser lit the tunnel around Sam. A fraction of a second later a pellet slammed into one of the rats in the front row.

Sam saw panic set in as the furry mass shrank back and folded in on itself.

But he was wrong. It wasn't panic. It was bloodlust.

Tiny fangs flashed in the light as the mob attacked their wounded comrade.

Sam backed away from the carnage and turned off the flashlight for five seconds. When he flicked it back on, the scene looked exactly the same. It seemed like a good sign. Maybe in their feeding frenzy they'd forgotten about him.

He headed away from the bridge as fast as he could safely go, checking behind him every couple of minutes. It appeared he'd made a clean break, but the fourth time he looked back, the flashlight caught a new front row of tiny glistening eyes following him silently down the path.

IN THE NEXT FEW HOURS SAM FORMED A routine. Move along the path as fast as he could and then, when the Cairo sewer space monsters were too close for comfort, he'd turn and take out a couple of the front row. This would trigger another feeding frenzy. Sometimes, one of the victims would drop into the canal, and a wave of bodies would pour in after it. They seemed just as capable of dismembering their friends in the water as they were on dry land. Sam learned to aim for targets near the wall. This created a rat traffic jam that slowed the group down.

The system seemed to be working. He still had plenty of ammo, since the magazine in the handle held hundreds of pellets. He was confident of making it to the exit point in time. But everything changed when a new sound drifted up the tunnel.

More creatures. These were coming toward him, and they were of the two-legged variety.

10

RAT FOOD

IT WAS A SOLITARY COUGH THAT HAD
given them away. If it hadn't been for that, Sam would
have walked right into them. They were coming out
of a cross-tunnel just ahead on the right. There'd been
no flashlight to signal their presence. They had their
hands full. But Sam didn't find that out till later.

It was the second to last intersection before the
truck depot. If he had gotten there even five minutes earlier, Sam would have been home free. Instead,
he had just a few seconds to act. Going back wasn't
an option. The brown horde had made sure of that.
There were two bridges at the intersection ahead.
One went left, one straight ahead. Sam considered

making a run for it, but really, there was only one way to go.

Sounds of heavy breathing and scuffing boots filled the chamber as Sam lowered himself into the water, but his feet weren't touching the bottom. Hanging off the edge of the path, his fingers would show up like little meat signposts if flashlights were switched on. He took a breath, shut his eyes, and let go.

It was a quick and silent fall, but not without cost. Sam had tucked the gun into his belt. As he landed, it fell out, lost forever in the black soup that was up to his chest. All he could do was push himself against the wall and wait.

The beams from two flashlights bounced off the walls. The bridge across the canal Sam was standing in groaned as one of the men walked out to the middle and lit a cigarette. Sam was dangerously in the open. It would take only a brief wave of a flashlight to expose him. He decided to risk moving under the bridge.

Sam sank down till his nose was just above the surface. The stench of stagnant water and decaying matter filled his nostrils. He tried to block out thoughts of where he was and what he was soaking in and focus on getting under the cover of the bridge.

Suddenly, it sounded like heavy raindrops were hitting the water behind him. It was great timing. The noise turned into a downpour, drowning out Sam's movements. He reached cover and turned to view the spectacle. A thousand hungry eyes had followed him into the canal. The surface was so thick with rodents, it looked like you could have walked across them. From the bridge it must have looked impressive. For Sam, down at water level and knowing he was the target, the sight was terrifying. There was a burst of excited Egyptian chatter from the man, and the bridge began to creak as the second man, dragging cargo behind him, joined the other. Thoughts of the oncoming rats were forgotten as Sam had visions of the rusty old structure buckling under the weight and crashing down on him. But those thoughts lasted only until the two flashlights lit up the rats again. Their collective swimming efforts had churned up the sewer. It looked like five hundred black and brown socks in a washing machine.

More Egyptian was spoken; then the bridge began to sway as the two men called out together. *"Talata, etneen, wahid!"* It was a countdown. A couple of seconds of silence ended with a loud watery explosion.

The giggles of delight sounded oddly out of place as the two men inspected their handiwork. It was chaos. The tightly packed rat swim team had had their formation shattered. Tiny bodies were bobbing up and down, unable to handle the waves that had been kicked up. But what got Sam's attention was the source of the splash: There was a new body floating in the middle of the sewer.

But this one was much bigger and wearing clothes.

SAM WATCHED WITH SICK FASCINATION as the rats went to work on their floating buffet. As the feasting began, the events of the past few hours fell into place.

The rats hadn't been scared of him because they were used to seeing humans on their turf. Humans that brought food. The canal was an underground body dump. The rats were the cleanup team.

There was a shout from one of the men on the bridge; he'd spotted something sticking out of the corpse. In their eagerness to get at the flesh, the rats were ripping the clothing off with their claws and teeth. The frenzy had exposed a wallet, and the discovery was important enough for one of the men to cross to the other side of the canal to try to retrieve it. Sam slipped farther back into the shadows.

When it became obvious the man couldn't reach the body from the path, he gave up and, much to his companion's amusement, lowered himself into the canal and waded out toward the floating mass of soggy fur balls. Using the flashlight as a club, he belted the rats out of the way, grabbed the wallet, and waved it triumphantly at his colleague. Caught in the flashlight from the bridge, the wallet was covered in so much blood it looked like it had been pulled out of the victim's chest, not his pocket. The blood dribbled down the man's arm as he held his prize in the air. Without realizing it, he'd turned himself into a new item on the menu.

Using the dead body as a springboard, a couple of the more energetic rodents leapt through the air and latched on to the man's exposed forearm. He howled and swatted one of his attackers with his flashlight. Suddenly, the whole mob wanted in on the action. Rats began launching themselves at the terrified Egyptian, who dropped the wallet and began swatting rats as if they were mutant mosquitoes. His cries of distress were enough to stop his companion's laughter and bring him down off the bridge. He wasn't game enough to get into the water, but he lay on the path and held his arm out, using his flashlight to give him extra reach. Sam was so engrossed in the rescue attempt he didn't realize the flashlight was aimed straight at him until it was too late. There was a grunt of surprise from the man on the path. Sam could see what was going through his mind: He was torn between his instinct to go after the intruder and helping his friend. Luckily for Sam the decision was made for the man when his rat-covered partner lunged toward him, and suddenly he was fighting to avoid being pulled into the water as well.

Sam didn't waste a second of his reprieve. He turned and began wading down the murky canal, determined to put as much distance between himself and the two body dumpers as he could.

THE HOWLS OF THE RAT ATTACK VICTIM bounced off the sewer walls, but that was good news for Sam. As long as the man was still in trouble, his mate would be with him. It was when things went quiet that the chase would start.

A few minutes later the sewer fell silent.

Sam pushed on in total blackness. Using his flashlight was out of the question, so he moved by feel, running his hand along the slimy brick wall. If he got up to the path, he could move faster, but to do that he had to get to a ladder before the men got to him.

A new sound drifted down the sewer. The now familiar squeaks of the rusty bridge.

The chase was on.

Sam stumbled as his hand hit open space. He'd reached the next intersection. A ladder was just ahead. As he crossed over, he could hear two sets of boots thumping along the path. Voices began calling out in low, angry tones. And then, as Sam's hand made contact with cold steel, a new problem hit him. The intersection had been the *last* intersection. This ladder was *the* ladder. The exit to the truck yards. If he climbed up to the path and tried to lose his tail, there was no way he'd make it back in time. He sank back into the water. Better to wait there and hope they passed by.

As Sam watched the two flashlight beams come dancing down the path, he noticed they kept stopping and turning away. They were checking the water. Sam's choice had been made for him. He had to move.

THE TWO MEN STOPPED AT THE LADDER. The wet one slumped against the wall, breathing heavily, while the other peered over the edge of the path. When he was done, he moved off, calling out to his partner, who got to his feet reluctantly and shuffled up the path. Sam watched all this from his hiding place high above them.

As he was climbing up onto the path, Sam realized he had one more option—to hide at the top of the ladder and hope his trackers didn't bother looking up.

The danger passed by, and Sam pulled his cell phone out of his pocket, thankful he'd put it and his sketch book in the plastic bag the gun had come in, to protect them from getting wet. The green glow of the screen lit up the concrete chamber around him. The good news was it was five to six. The bad news followed quickly. The sounds of the men returning.

The blackness at Sam's feet began to lighten as the flashlights got closer. Perhaps they had given up and were going home. But as the circular patch of light below grew brighter, Sam saw things were about to go very bad.

During his time huddled at the top of the ladder, the steady drip from his waterlogged clothing had created a huge wet stain on the path below. Sam could tell from the way the flashlight stuck to the puddle that the men had spotted it. He pushed the iron lid above him. It didn't budge. Two dark shapes appeared below, and the narrow shaft Sam had climbed filled with light. Angry cries bounced off the walls, and the ladder began to shake.

Sam was trapped like a rat. All he could do was watch as one of the killers came for him, his black bulk silhouetted by his companion's flashlight below.

The flashlight! Sam pulled it from his pocket and hurled it down the shaft. The *thud* of metal on flesh triggered a stream of harshly spoken Egyptian, but the figure kept climbing. Sam locked his arms tightly around the top rung of the ladder as a probing hand brushed his shoe. He kicked wildly, connecting with something soft and triggering another burst of Egyptian curses. Then a hand grabbed him by the ankle and tried to pull him off the ladder. Sam kicked with his free leg, but lost his footing on the slippery rung. Now the only things stopping him from plunging down the shaft were his arms, still hugging the top of the ladder. The man below kept pulling and tugging downward. Sam's grip was slipping. Gravity and the Egyptian body dumper were about to win the battle.

"Give me your hand!" ordered a gruff voice.

Right at that second Sam didn't have a spare hand to give. He couldn't even lift his head up to see who was speaking. He'd been so focused on fighting off the man below, he hadn't noticed the sewer lid slide back.

The man above didn't ask again. Instead, two large hands slipped under Sam's armpits, hauled him out of the hole, and dumped him on the ground as easily as if he'd been a small sack of potatoes.

Lying there in the predawn darkness, Sam watched as an elderly but well-built man pushed the lid back into position and rolled a large rock on top of it. Muffled thumps of fists on steel broke out on the other side of the manhole cover.

"You wanna say good-bye to your friends?" inquired

Sam's rescuer. Sam shook his head wildly, which amused the large Egyptian. "Okay, then. We go." He pointed to the battered old truck parked a few feet away. "But you know . . . after a few hours in that, you might wish you were back down in the sewer."

Sam didn't think that was likely.

11

SHIPPING NEWS

ALTHOUGH HE HADN'T INTRODUCED HIM-
self, the man Sam assumed was Kareem led him to the
back of the truck, swung one of the large metal doors
open, and motioned for him to get in.

"Guess I'm traveling economy class," Sam muttered.

The space was filled with large cardboard boxes.
The biggest contained a fridge. It wasn't Sam's knowledge of kitchen product packaging that told him this,
but the words scrawled on one side with a black marker.
Kareem coughed impatiently, making it clear that he
was waiting for Sam to sit down and get comfortable

before he shut the door. Well, not comfortable, thought Sam. That was impossible. At least economy class on an aircraft came with a pillow and a blanket.

Kareem slammed the door shut and it became obvious why he'd been waiting. The back of the truck was now pitch-black. It was like being down in the sewer again. Minus the water, the rats, and men carrying a dead body. The engine rumbled to life and the heavy scent of diesel wafted through the wooden floorboards. But Sam didn't care. It had been a night from hell, the third in a row, and he was exhausted. Kareem nudged the truck out onto the street and before he had it up to third gear, his passenger was asleep.

SAM WOKE THINKING KAREEM HAD TURNED a light on. It turned out to be the sun, streaming through a small skylight in the roof. But that wasn't what had woken him. It was the silence.

The truck had stopped.

Sam felt like he had been asleep for hours, but the cell phone told him it was only just after seven. The sunroof lit the space like a weak lightbulb, but as he looked around, Sam spotted three smaller light sources coming from the back door. Tiny holes that looked suspiciously as if they'd been made by bullets. One of them, conveniently created at head height, made the perfect peephole. The first thing Sam saw when he looked through it was the imposing shape of the truck driver lumbering toward him with a plastic bag. Sam darted back to his spot by the fridge as the door opened.

"Here . . . for you," Kareem said. The bag kicked up small clouds of dust as it skidded across the floorboards.

Sam's eyes widened as he saw the contents. Water, a chocolate bar, and chips. "Thanks," he said, but the door was already slamming shut. Sam sensed Kareem wasn't too happy to be carrying human cargo.

SAM WAS JUST FINISHING HIS BREAKFAST of champions when the truck stopped again. This time, when the door opened, Kareem was holding a microwave oven.

"What do you want with alchemy?" he asked as he slid the box into the truck.

"Alchemy. What's that?" asked Sam

"Those symbols," said Kareem, pointing to the piece of paper with the triangles. "They're alchemy symbols. Earth, air, water, fire."

Even though Sam had stored his clues in the plastic bag, they had still managed to get damp, so he had laid them out on the floor of the truck to dry.

Kareem pulled a pen from his pocket. "Here, I write them down for you."

"What is alchemy exactly?" asked Sam as Kareem
scribbled under the triangles.

EARTH   AIR   FIRE   WATER

"Gold—that's what it's about. Turning lead into
gold." Kareem smiled. "You wonder how I know about
alchemy?" Sam didn't. He was trying to work out how
this new information fit into his uncle's disappearance.
"When I am young and stupid I think I will get rich
quick by making gold from lead."

"Did it work?"

Kareem shook his head. "Of course not. Now I am
old and stupid and I get rich very, very slowly by driving
truck." This last admission seemed more for his own
benefit than Sam's, but the conversation had softened
the old man a fraction. "I make a few more stops, okay?"
he said as he swung the door closed. "Then I take you
to Al Minya."

Despite the thaw in the relationship, Sam wasn't
invited to sit up front. As more stops were made, he was
left in the back with his sketchbook and his thoughts.
If alchemy was about gold, was gold the secret behind
Jasper's mission? That might explain the metal detector. As the day wore on, the back of the truck warmed

up. By the time Sam finished his drawing of the sewer rats, the car horns and street babble of Cairo had subsided, leaving only the monotonous roar of the truck's engine as it powered down the open road.

SAM WAS ASLEEP AGAIN WHEN MARY rang.

"Hi, it's me. Did I wake you again?"

"No," he lied.

"I got your text last night. Did you get away okay?"

Sam grinned. He could afford to now that the terrors of the sewer were behind him. "Yeah. I got away okay."

"So where are you now?" Mary sounded concerned. "Sam, you know I would have helped you get to Amarna."

"I know. Look, Mary . . . I'm in this, and I have no choice. But I don't want to get you into trouble." Sam didn't bother adding that he was still just a little suspicious of Mary's eagerness to help him.

"It's no trouble, Sam. I want to help. I'm bored here in Cairo anyway. Where are you now?"

As soon as he mentioned Al Minya, she cut him off.

"Al Minya. That's interesting. That's why I was calling you. Bassem's friend went to the Port Records office in Alexandria. He greased a few palms with silver, which is the way you get things done in Egypt, and he found out your uncle was only interested in ships that sailed from Cairo to Al Minya."

"Well, that's great. That's where I'm headed."

"I know," said Mary, "but here's the strange bit. He was only interested in ships from 1942."

"Nineteen forty-two." Sam repeated it slowly. It felt familiar for some reason, but before he had a chance to take it further, his thoughts were interrupted by a dull beeping sound coming from his phone.

"Mary, look, sorry, I'm going to have to go."

There was a moment of silence before Mary spoke. "Sam Force. You're making a habit of cutting me off."

"No, no, it's not like that. It's my phone. The battery is running low."

"I should have thought of that," replied Mary. "Given you a spare or something. Sorry."

"That's okay, but I need to conserve the power. This is the only way we can stay in touch." Despite not wanting to get Mary more involved in his troubles, the idea of being cut off from her was a daunting prospect. He was unsure of her motivations, but he *was* sure that she'd been a big help so far. "Let's just text till I can get a new battery."

Mary didn't sound convinced. "How are you going to do that?"

"I'm not sure. Maybe Kareem can help me."

"Who's Kareem? Honestly, Sam, for a guy who doesn't have any friends in Egypt, you seem pretty popular."

Sam laughed. "Look, I'll talk . . . I mean *text* soon, okay?"

"Cool," said Mary. The line went dead.

Getting a new battery was important, but there was something more pressing. Sam pulled out the first clue he'd found: Panehesy, one thousand, nine hundred and forty-two. Written out as a word he hadn't recognized it as a date, but after the conversation with Mary it seemed obvious. Jasper wasn't interested in Akhenaten's high priest. He was searching for a ship that had traveled up the Nile in 1942.

Sam let out a yell of delight and punched the box beside him. The clues were revealing themselves. He was a long way from understanding the full picture, but he was heading in the right direction. He was sure of that.

FIFTEEN MINUTES LATER THE TRUCK pulled into a gas station, and Sam seized the chance to deal with his dying phone battery. As Kareem filled the tank, Sam called out to him, asking if he had a cable to charge a mobile from his cigarette lighter. The man said he didn't, so Sam asked to be allowed to go and buy one. It took all his negotiating skills, mixed with some good old-fashioned whining, to talk Kareem into letting him out of the truck. The fact that the place was empty, combined with Sam's thinly veiled threats of also badly needing to use the restroom, convinced the grumpy driver to open the back door.

He was down to his last twenty bucks. Sam had no idea if it was enough for a mobile phone charger cable, but a quick look around the dingy shop told him his chances of finding one were remote anyway.

The shelves held the bare necessities for man and machine. A few cans of oil, packets of spark plugs, rice, soup, and cigarettes. The only thing there seemed to be plenty of were free brochures that were jammed into racks against the window.

Sam waited for the woman behind the counter to get off the phone. There was a chance she might have some mobile phone accessories stored in the back.

Despite the fact the phone conversation was in Egyptian, the girl's tone told Sam the call wasn't work related. After trying unsuccessfully to get her attention, Sam realized he would have to wait for the call to run its course, so he took a look at the wall of brochures. They were mostly for motels. All of them were cashing in on Egypt's famous past with stupid names like the Sphinx Inn, King Tut's Motel, the Mighty Nefertiti, and Pharaoh Palms.

"Can I help you? Hello? Boy. I said, can I help you?"

Sam heard the woman behind the counter the second time. The verbal exchange that followed was short and sweet. No, they didn't sell phone accessories, but as Sam hurried back to the truck, he went with something much more valuable.

The answer to another clue.

THE SUN HAD SET AND SAM WAS BACK IN darkness when the high-pitched beeping woke him. The green glow coming from his phone told him a text had arrived.

SAM. THE POLICE KNOW YOU ARE ON THAT TRUCK. THEY ARE COMING FOR YOU!

Sam stared at the message until the screen switched off. Sitting there in his vibrating black box, he tried to kick-start his head. The police? Why? How?

He pushed a button on the phone to light the screen again. The battery reading was at 2 percent. Did he risk a call to Mary to find out more?

He didn't. Instead, he used the glow to guide him down to the bullet peephole.

Small dots of yellow light betrayed the presence of cars and trucks stretching for miles behind. They were on a long, straight road. Surely he'd be able to see trouble coming.

And then he did.

It was a long way off. Perhaps it had been behind a truck, and that's why he hadn't spotted it straightaway, but now the small blue flashing light stood out in contrast to the weak yellow line it was weaving its way through.

The police were coming for him, and he was locked in the back of a moving truck with nowhere to run.

Sam ran anyway, to the front of the truck, banged on the wall, and called out for Kareem to stop.

He either didn't hear or chose not to.

The truck rolled on.

Another text arrived. SAM. YOU HAVE TO GET ON THE ROOF.

What was she talking about?

The truck lurched, and Sam smashed against one of the boxes. The impact sent the phone flying out of his hand and into the corner. When he retrieved it, another text had arrived: GET ON THE ROOF, SAM. NOW!!!!!!

As he stared at the row of exclamation marks, the first faint sounds of the police car siren reached him. Then the screen went black. The battery was dead.

Get on the roof. Why? How?

The *how* hit Sam in the head. Literally. One of the smaller boxes that had been sitting on top of the fridge slid off as Kareem veered into a new lane.

The boxes. Of course. He could build a stairway up

to the sunroof. Only problem was, he would have to do it fast and in total darkness.

Sam groped his way toward the front of the truck where he remembered seeing a box containing an oven. He slid it next to the fridge and used it to get up, taking the microwave with him.

The whole unit wobbled as Kareem changed lanes yet again. The guy was suddenly driving like he was on a slalom ski course, and Sam wondered if it had something to do with the boys in blue behind them.

It was time for the final stage of the escape plan. Sam couldn't reach the sunroof from the top of the fridge. He needed a bit of extra height. That was where the microwave came in. It was small and unstable, and if Kareem chose to make an evasive maneuver in the next thirty seconds, things would go very bad. But crouched there in the darkness, Sam knew there was no point trying to second-guess the big guy up front, so he went for it.

The fridge had been almost directly under the sunroof. By Sam's reckoning, with the microwave dead center, all he had to do was get on it and reach up. He reckoned wrong. Sam's hands touched the smooth metal of the roof, then the truck drifted slightly to one side. It wasn't much, but with nothing to hold, Sam toppled over.

He landed heavily on a corner of the fridge box where the point dug into his shoulder. It felt like he'd been stabbed. Sam cried out as he slipped off the fridge. He hit the oven headfirst and the dark interior of the truck filled with stars. But he knew he'd been lucky. The oven had broken his fall. If he'd gone all the way to the floor, his escape attempt would have ended there.

With his head spinning and bolts of pain shooting through him, Sam considered giving the whole thing up. Was the risk worth it? How was getting onto the roof of a speeding truck going to help? He had almost run out of time anyway. The bleating siren told him the police were closing in fast.

In the end, Sam decided if he was going to go down, he would do it trying to escape. He got back on top of the fridge, moved the microwave close to the edge, and stepped up.

This time, grabbing hands made contact with the frame of the sunroof.

Sam ran his fingers around the edge until he found the two screws holding it in place. He undid them, and the plastic panel swung down. Now all he had to do was get through it.

Even using the microwave, it was still a stretch to the sunroof. Sam could get his arms through, but not quite far enough to pull himself up. He was about to jump up when the truck swerved across three lanes toward an off-ramp. The move sent the boxes under Sam's feet toppling over, leaving him hanging from the roof like a human chandelier. He dug his fingers into the frame of the sunroof, but he was slipping. In a matter of seconds he'd fall.

The truck swerved back the other way as Kareem straightened it up. The motion swung Sam like a pendulum. He felt himself rising up, and as he did he seized the opportunity to shove his elbows through the sunroof. It was a tight fit, and as Sam wriggled out onto the roof of the truck, he discovered he was swapping a precarious situation for an even worse one.

The interior of the truck had been an island of calm compared to the gale-force winds now blasting him in the face. Kareem had taken them off the motorway, but he hadn't slowed down. The frame of sunroof was the only thing stopping Sam from being blown to his death. Despite the roar of the wind Sam could still hear the high-pitched whine of the siren. The police car had followed them up the off-ramp. There was no way Kareem didn't know he was being followed now, but Sam didn't think it was his loyalty to his passenger that had prompted the getaway attempt. Maybe there was more to the kitchen appliances than met the eye.

The truck picked up speed, making it even harder

for Sam to keep a grip. He had made it onto the roof, but why? What on earth had Mary been thinking? Surely she didn't expect him to jump. Even if he made it without breaking his neck, the police were so close now they would see him.

The wind was getting stronger. But weirdly, Sam noticed, it now seemed to be coming at him from every direction. The noise was changing as well. The roar of the wind was starting to sound almost mechanical. Curiosity and fear forced Sam to risk raising his head so he could get a better look behind.

The police car was gone. Well, not gone, but Sam's view of it had been blocked.

And now he knew why he'd been told to get on the roof.

Just a few feet behind the truck and a little higher off the ground than Sam, was Mary, sitting in a big plastic bubble.

12

COME FLY WITH ME

THE WAY SAM SAW IT, THERE WAS A good chance he was about to be hacked to death by the rotors of a helicopter. He tried to take some comfort from the fact that Mary, sitting in the cockpit, didn't seem too worried. But she wasn't the one pinned to the roof of a speeding truck.

The chopper rose above head-chopping height and drifted over the truck. The side door opened and a flimsy metal ladder rolled out. Mary was in the doorway, urging Sam to climb up. What he felt like screaming at her was: *No! You come down!*

With one hand locked to the frame of the sunroof,

Sam made a grab for the ladder, but it whipped past, just out of arm's reach. Fighting against the wind, he got onto his knees and tried again. The ladder swung and twisted around him as if they were playing a game of tag. Balancing on a few boxes suddenly seemed like child's play.

The chopper backed off, straightened up, and came in again directly from behind. This was it. Sam knew he wouldn't get a better chance. As the ladder drifted over the back of the truck, he let go of the sunroof and committed both hands to the capture.

He'd been so focused on the ladder, Sam hadn't noticed that the police car had overtaken the truck. It pulled ahead, then swerved in front of the truck, forcing Kareem to hit the brakes. This happened just as Sam grabbed for the ladder. The truck's sudden drop in speed meant the ladder came at Sam faster than he had been expecting. Rather than grabbing it neatly with two hands, one of the rungs smashed into his nose, and the ladder continued past him.

Sam threw his hands up for protection. It was an instinctive move and a lucky one, because as the bottom of the ladder swept past, his hands caught the last rung.

Sam's arms felt like they were being pulled out of their sockets as he was ripped off the roof of the truck. Barely aware of what was happening, Sam clung to the ladder. He caught a glimpse of the truck and police car below, then blackness as the helicopter left the road and moved out into the desert.

Sam swung through the dark on the end of the ladder like a trapeze artist. He might have even enjoyed the thrill if he hadn't been losing his grip. And he didn't have the strength to pull himself up. All he could do was hold on and pray the helicopter landed quickly.

His eyes were shut tight because of the wind blasting him in the face, so when the hand grabbed him, he freaked out. He hadn't felt the ladder being winched up, and he opened his eyes as Mary pulled him into the chopper. Sam fell back on the bench seat as Mary slid the door shut.

"You look terrible," she yelled above the noise of the helicopter turbines.

In the dim cabin light Sam surveyed the carnage. His face and shirt were covered in blood thanks to the whack on the nose from the ladder. He looked like a victim from a B-grade slasher movie. "It's not as bad as it looks," he said.

Mary pulled a small first aid kit from under the seat and took out a packet of wet wipes. "Sorry, that's all I have right now."

Sam ignored them. "Mary, what just happened?"

He knew she'd heard him, but instead of answering,

she opened the packet herself and began trying to wipe some of the blood off Sam's shirt. He should have been grateful. After all, she'd just saved him. But the whole situation was way too weird.

Her cleaning efforts started to annoy him. He shoved her hand away. "I don't need to get clean, Mary. I want answers!"

Mary looked hurt by his outburst, but Sam didn't care. He wanted to understand what was going on. "How did you find me?"

"Your mobile," said Mary. "We tracked the signal. Sam, I wanted to help. I still do."

"And you just happened to have a helicopter standing by?" Sam's head was spinning. He felt like he was seeing Mary for the first time.

"Sam, we're going to land in a minute, and I'll explain everything then, I promise."

That was good news, because Sam had just realized he was about to throw up.

THE LIGHTS OF A SMALL TOWN APPEARED in the distance. Sam guessed it was Al Minya. He didn't know if it was the whack on the nose or the escape from the speeding truck, but he knew there was no way he would be able to hold on that long. Thankfully, seconds later, the chopper plunged into a gully. Making a hurried excuse about needing to take a leak, Sam kicked the door open and jumped out. It was only then he registered that the pilot was Mary's Egyptian minder, Bassem.

Sam stumbled blindly across the stony ground, not waiting for his eyes to adjust to the darkness. Waves of nausea rolled through his head, but all he could think about was getting far enough away so Mary and Bassem wouldn't hear him being sick.

A boot-sized boulder brought Sam's journey to an ungainly end. He tripped and landed face-first. What he expected next was vomit, but instead he lay there, head throbbing as if he'd just gone a few rounds with a heavyweight boxer. After a couple of minutes the nausea passed. All Sam could hear was the sound of his breathing, short, labored breaths like he'd just run a marathon or jumped from a moving truck onto a ladder dangling from a helicopter.

When he finally sat up, Sam realized he was lost. The total blackness of the desert had swallowed the chopper, and he had no idea which direction he'd come from. The easiest thing would have been to call out for Mary, but Sam was too proud for that. He wanted to get back and find out what was going on, but he wasn't going to call out like a nervous kid.

He got to his feet and moved slowly in the direction

he thought he had come from. It turned out to be a decent guess, because seconds later a tiny ball of light appeared up ahead. The flame from Bassem's match lit his face for only an instant, but it was enough for Sam to get his bearings. As he increased his pace, he was glad he'd kept his mouth shut, and a few moments later he was even more thankful.

He covered the ground more cautiously than he had on the outward journey. A gentle breeze was blowing down the gully from the chopper, bringing with it the scent of Bassem's cigarette along with the familiar tones of Mary's voice. She was quietly talking on the cell phone, almost in a whisper. It made Sam stop and drop to his knees. Why would she do that out here in the middle of nowhere? Unless it was *Sam* who wasn't meant to hear. . . .

Sam strained to try to pick up her conversation. He caught only a few fragments, but it was enough.

"No, I don't think he suspects a thing. . . . He's leading us straight to his uncle."

As Sam got to his feet, he was suddenly aware of the excruciatingly loud crunching sounds the stones under his shoes were making. Keeping his eyes focused in the direction of Mary's voice, he began walking backward. It was too dark to run, but the voice in Sam's head was screaming at him to get away from that helicopter as fast as he could.

"Sam, are you okay?" Mary's voice boomed out through the blackness. Then a thick beam of light erupted from nearby. Bassem was using a searchlight. Luckily, he'd aimed it in the wrong direction.

Now Sam ran. He did it at a half crouch, his arms out in front to stop him from running into trees and rocks. Behind him he heard Mary yelling his name. With every step he expected the searchlight to swing down the gully and lock on to him, but it didn't. The reason became apparent as the chopper's engines whined to life.

Sam ran on, desperate for some kind of cover. As his eyes adjusted to the darkness, he made out small objects, but nothing that was any use to him. The chopper's engines reached maximum speed, and the abrupt change in sound told Sam it had lifted off. Time was running out.

Just ahead the gully opened out into a large, flat area. Sam ran on till he hit ankle-deep mud, tripped, and fell.

The large, flat area he'd seen was the Nile River.

As he extracted himself from the slimy river gunk, Sam looked back to see the lights of the helicopter drift up over the hill toward Al Minya. He'd bought himself some time, but it wouldn't take them long to work out he hadn't gone that way.

Sam spotted the outline of a tree trunk farther along the riverbank. He considered searching for something else, but the sound of the helicopter returning killed that idea.

Bassem retraced his flight path, then cruised slowly down the gully. He drifted out over the river, turned, and used the spotlight to sweep the bank. It didn't take him long to zero in on the log.

The chopper nosed forward for a closer look. Loose stones and sand were kicked up as it circled slowly around the rotting log, but there was no sign of life.

After that, Bassem and Mary seemed to lose interest. The helicopter flew up and down the river's edge one more time before banking sharply and powering off into the night.

The log had been an obvious hiding place. That's why Sam had known Bassem would check it out, and that's why he'd known he couldn't hide anywhere near it. Instead, he'd gone underground. Well, under the mud. It hadn't taken long to dig a shallow trench and then pile the mud back over himself, leaving just a small hole for his nose.

Sam lay there listening to the sound of the chopper

fading away. He was surprised they'd given up so easily. Were they going for reinforcements? The thought propelled Sam from his slimy grave. He waded into the river to wash the mud and blood off himself. Sunrise was still a few hours away, but it would take a while to get into town. Mary and Bassem knew he was headed downstream to Al Minya, but he had no choice. That was where his uncle had gone, and that was where he had to go to pick up his trail. Sam was just glad he'd listened to his instincts and not told Mary exactly where he was heading.

She had been playing him all along.

Sam gave up the cleanup attempt and dove into the Nile. Why walk? The river was going the same way he needed to. As he drifted in the gentle current, Sam's mind drifted farther, back to the Charles River in Boston.

Sam had joined the rowing squad as a way to get off the school grounds, but out on the water he had found a new kind of freedom. On the early morning training sessions, in his one-man craft, he felt like he could keep rowing all the way to Boston Harbor and beyond. It wasn't about escaping from school; it was the feeling that his life hadn't turned out the way it was meant to. Out on the water he felt like he had the power to change everything if he just kept going. And now, lying there in the cool embrace of the Nile, he felt that same sense of calm. Calm that came from knowing he was on the right path. That everything would work out. Mary might have known which town he was heading to, but it was a big place. It would be hard to find someone unless you knew exactly where to look. Thanks to the stop for gasoline, Sam knew exactly where to look, so he lay still and let the Nile carry him down to Al Minya, and to room 18 of the Nefertiti Motel.

13
WE WERE EXPECTING YOU

SAM SPENT HALF OF HIS SOGGY CASH ON an I LOVE EGYPT T-shirt, a cheap knockoff of an Adidas sports bag, and two newspapers. He saved the rest for a taxi.

Sitting by the Nile in the early morning sun waiting for his pants to dry, it had occurred to Sam that the best way to get to the Nefertiti Motel was by taxi. The driver would know exactly where to go, and turning up by taxi would also add to the illusion he wanted to create. Plus, it would keep him off the streets—and out of Mary's sight.

Al Minya seemed to be a miniature version of Cairo,

with rows and rows of mismatched concrete buildings desperately in need of a wash or a new coat of paint.

As the taxi rattled down the narrow streets, Sam tried to tap back into some of the confidence he'd felt floating down the Nile the night before. For a while he'd felt invincible, as if nothing and no one could stop him from getting to his uncle. But now, in the harsh light of day in the back of the taxi, the hopelessness of his situation seemed to crowd back in on him.

Sam fingered the metal scarab beetle hanging around his neck. The last time he'd been in a taxi had been with Hadi, the last person he had truly been able to trust. Mary's betrayal had hit him hard. He'd liked her. A lot. He had taken her help at face value. The idea that she had been using him cut deep. It also brought home to Sam just what he was up against. He was collecting an ever growing list of enemies. The police, the man with the beard in his uncle's apartment, the man who'd been waiting downstairs, and now Mary and her silent giant. But where did they all fit in? What could his uncle be onto that was so important?

Sam tried to work this through in his mind, but the black clouds of despair just grew darker. He wound down the window and earned a sharp scowl from the driver as the outside heat diluted the cool of the cab. Sam didn't care. He pushed his head out, and hot wind blasted his face. He had to snap himself out of this mood. Burn away the traces of the tears he could feel forming. He was about to check into a motel as a young, seasoned traveler. He wasn't going to lose it and wander in looking like a crybaby.

A BRIEF LOOK AROUND THE DRAB LITTLE reception area told Sam that the brochure for the Mighty Nefertiti Motel that he'd seen at the gas station had been made a long time ago. Possibly during the reign of Nefertiti herself. And judging by the wrinkles on the face of the woman eyeing Sam from behind the counter, she had probably known the great queen personally.

"Can I help you?" she asked in a tone that let Sam know that she thought it was highly unlikely.

Sam had gone in trying to project the image of a well-traveled man of the world checking into yet another motel, but he suspected she saw him for what he was: a nervous young kid holding a bag stuffed with newspaper to make it look full.

"I . . ." Sam searched for the words, but they didn't come. Meanwhile, the woman's eyebrows began to rise higher and higher up her forehead as she awaited his explanation. "I-I . . . ," he stammered again. "My uncle . . . Jasper. He told me to come here."

It was risky, throwing Jasper's name out like that. If the police or other people on Sam's trail had beaten him here, this woman would know he was the one they were looking for. But it seemed to have a positive effect on the old lady. Her face softened a fraction as she spoke. "Professor Jasper? You are with the professor?"

Sam nodded. It seemed his uncle had made an attempt to disguise his identity. "Yes. I'm his nephew. I mean student . . . his student."

The woman banged on the door behind her, then yelled with the kind of volume Sam wouldn't have guessed she was capable of. "Ahmed! Ahmed, come!"

The door creaked open to reveal a man who looked as old as the woman and in even worse repair.

"We have a visitor, Ahmed. This boy is with the professor."

Ahmed didn't appear quite as excited by the news as the old lady did, but he picked up the key she'd slid across the counter and shuffled to the stairs in the corner, motioning for Sam to follow him.

It was an agonizingly slow trip up the stairs and along a balcony that looked over the parking lot. The Mighty Nefertiti wasn't a big place; Sam could have easily found room 18 himself, but he was forced to shuffle behind one of the world's slowest bellboys. It wasn't until they got to the door that Ahmed spoke.

"We were beginning to wonder about the professor," the old man mumbled as he attempted to get the key in the lock.

"What do you mean?" Sam asked, trying to sound as casual as possible.

Ahmed got the key in on this third attempt. "We haven't seen him since Saturday," he said, pushing the door open. "He has yet to pay."

Now the woman's reaction to Sam's arrival made more sense. They'd been worried Jasper had done a runner.

"Perhaps you're paying for the room now?" inquired Ahmed, confirming Sam's suspicions.

Sam squeezed past him. "Ah yes, the professor is coming back later today," he said as he made a show of inspecting the room. "Tomorrow morning at the latest, and he said to tell you that he will be settling the bill in full then."

The look on Ahmed's face said he had expected to hear something like that. He left the key on the kitchen bench and shuffled back toward the stairs.

Sam sat on the edge of the bed. The room was almost as big as his uncle's apartment, and although he had only checked in on Thursday, Jasper had still managed to stamp his unique brand of messiness on it. Clothes and plates were scattered about. Only the table was clear, except for a phone that had been dragged to it from a small shelf on the wall, leaving the cord stretched across the room like a trip wire.

Sam fought the urge to lie back on the bed. That would have been the end of him. He was exhausted, and his body was crying out for sleep, but there was no time.

For a man as smart as Jasper, Sam knew he had zero imagination when it came to hiding places. Sure enough, tucked under the bed between the frame and mattress was a folded piece of paper that opened up to reveal a handmade map featuring the Nile and a series of upside-down triangles.

At least that's what Sam would have thought before his conversation with the truck driver. Now he knew they meant more.

In the middle of them was a new symbol. A new problem to be solved.

Sam hadn't expected his uncle to be at the Nefertiti, so he hadn't been let down, but he had hoped to find a better lead than an obscure map. He searched the rest of the room, checking all the obvious hiding places and some of the not so obvious ones in case his uncle had lifted his game. There was nothing. He didn't risk returning to the bed. The allure of sleep was far too strong. Instead, Sam sat at the table and planned his next move.

Food was fast becoming a priority. He hadn't eaten

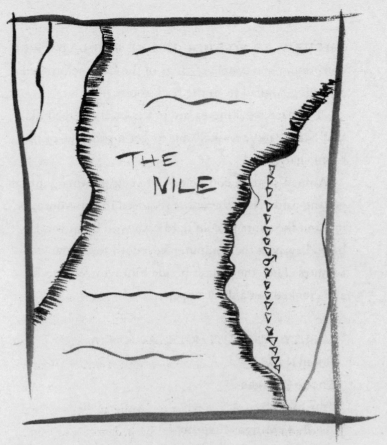

for nearly twenty-four hours. Sam wasn't surprised to find out the Nefertiti didn't do room service. Maybe that's why his uncle had brought the phone to the table. Or was there another reason? The Nefertiti didn't make money from food, but Sam was sure they charged their guests for phone calls. That meant he could find out exactly who Uncle Jasper had called and when.

★ ★ ★

THERE WAS NO SIGN OF THE OLD LADY AT reception, but a couple of rings of the brass bell roused the aging Ahmed from the back room.

"I've been speaking to my professor about the bill," said Sam, "and he asked me to get a printout of the room charges."

Ahmed seemed conflicted between the thought of getting paid versus the effort required to print out the bill, but the allure of cold hard cash won him over. He bashed away at the computer keyboard for a couple of minutes. Then the printer beside him whirred into life and cranked out a sheet of paper.

MIGHTY NEFERTITI MOTEL AL MINYA
Room No. 18
Phone Charges
Thu July 23
13:42—Al Minya Museum
Call dur 1.16
Charge—2NGP

Ahmed watched Sam fold the bill and put it in his pocket. "You are paying now?" he asked hopefully.

"I have to wait for the professor to return," Sam reminded him. "I thought I might do some sightseeing till he gets back. Can you tell me how to get to the Al Minya Museum?"

THE CULTURAL AND HISTORICAL FOUNDATION of Al Minya had a fancy name, but the building didn't live up to it. The two-story brick structure looked more like a warehouse, and it took three rings of the doorbell before he heard someone unlocking the door.

Standing in the doorway was a round-faced middle-aged woman wearing a beaming smile that revealed a set of teeth that seemed too big for her mouth. "Well, hello there, deary. Come on in."

Sam darted through the door, eager to get out of the sweltering midmorning heat. He didn't think to check if he was being watched.

Even if he had, it was unlikely he would have recognized the figure in sunglasses who had slipped into the coffee shop across the road.

14

BATHROOM BREAKOUT

IT WASN'T JUST THE FRIENDLY GREETING that had caught Sam off guard, it was the English accent.

"We're not open till two, my dear," said the woman, still with the oversized smile. "But we don't get many visitors even then, so you're welcome to have a look around."

They were standing in a large, dimly lit room full of glass cases that were filled with the standard museum fare—bits of old pottery, jewelry, and the odd stuffed animal. But Sam didn't care about any of that.

"What I'm really interested in is boats."

"Well, I'm afraid we don't have much in the way of boats, my dear, although there is a rather nice model of a pharaoh's royal yacht next to the cigarette machine."

"Sorry, I meant *old* boats. Ships. Ones that might have passed through here during World War Two."

The woman turned back to Sam, a sly grin on her face. "Oh, I see . . . 1942 in particular?"

Sam nodded. "That's right. Nineteen forty-two."

"You must be one of the professor's students," she said, striding off toward the wooden staircase in the middle of the room. "This way, dear. I'm Jenny Cole, by the way."

"Sam," he said as he raced to keep up. "When did you—"

"Arrive in Al Minya?"

Sam had been about to say, *last see the professor.*

"Affair of the heart brought me here, dear," she announced dramatically. "I came to marry the love of my life."

"So you've been here a long time," said Sam innocently.

Jenny tut-tutted at the comment. "Oh no. I met Habib last year . . . on the Internet."

"Oh . . . really." Sam tried not to sound too surprised. "That's cool." His response earned a cheerful laugh.

"Not really, dear. He did a runner on me after two

months. Took all my money and left me with the wedding debt and his gambling bills."

Sam had nothing to say to this, but Jenny continued her cheerful banter as they climbed the stairs. "So here I sit, on my lonesome in the desert, till I can pay my way out. Right . . . take a seat."

They had arrived at an old desk. The second floor of the museum was even dingier than downstairs. It reminded Sam of a mad professor's library. A solitary lightbulb struggled to light the room because the windows were blocked by shelves, which were packed with books and documents.

"The town records of Al Minya," said Jenny. "Bit of a nightmare, I'm afraid, but luckily I know exactly what you're after."

The smiling museum curator disappeared down one of the rows and returned carrying a battered leather book. "This is what the professor spent his time going through. The port records of all vessels that passed through Al Minya in '42." She dropped the book on the desk. "I hope you know which parts he was interested in, deary, because I have no idea." Jenny looked up with a glint in her eye. "I don't suppose the professor is back in town?"

Sam had to think quickly. "No . . . no, he isn't. He asked me to follow up on some of his research."

"Pity. He's quite a looker, isn't he?" Jenny smiled slyly. "Happily married, I suppose?"

The conversation had taken an awkward twist. Sam got it back on track. "I'm actually interested in one ship in particular. The *Panehesy*."

"Right, then. Let's have a look, shall we," said Jenny. "The *Panehesy* . . . the *Panehesy*," she muttered to herself as she flicked through the pages. "Ah yes, here it is."

Port of Al Minya   Shipping Records 1942

June 17

PANEHESY—25-ton merchant ship Reg 566892,
Sinclair Shipping

Docked 11.45 Wharf 2 En route from Amarna
delivering medical supplies.

DAMAGE REPORT—The Panehesy is leaking oil.
Captain reports explosion in boiler room that
has put a hole in the hull.

I have ordered the ship upstream to a mooring
barge to effect temporary repairs. Due to depart
tomorrow morning (June 18) for Alexandria.

"It's a good thing the *Panehesy* only stayed one night," said Jenny as Sam read the entry.

"Why is that?"

"Well . . ." Jenny had the look of someone about to share a good piece of gossip. "The night of June 18, 1942, a big storm hit Al Minya. Storm of the century. It lasted five days and buried half the town in sand. It actually altered the course of the Nile in some places."

"I don't understand," said Sam. "Why was it good luck for the *Panehesy*?"

"The mooring barge was lost in the storm. The *Panehesy* was the last ship to use it."

"Lost—what does that mean?"

"The barge was anchored in a channel between a small island and the bank of the Nile. Apparently, the storm filled in the channel and turned the island into just another bend in the river."

"So if the *Panehesy* had still been moored at the barge . . ."

"It would have been buried by the desert. See what I mean? A lucky escape."

Sam knew he was onto something crucial. "Where was the barge located?"

Jenny frowned at the logbook. "The next page has been ripped out. I can't think why someone would do that."

Sam did. It was his uncle covering his tracks. "Could this be the location?" he asked, pulling Jasper's hand-drawn map from his pocket.

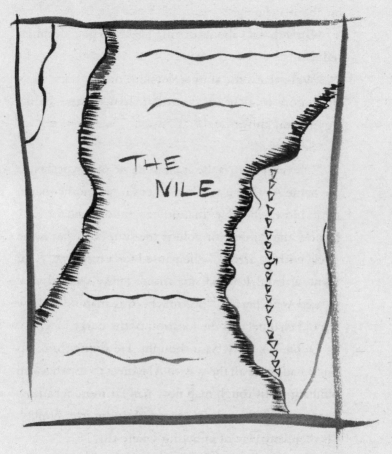

"Deary, that's not much of a map. I mean, it could be anywhere on the Nile."

"I know, but these upside-down triangles . . . they're

the alchemy sign for water, aren't they? That could show where the river used to run before the storm."

"Interesting theory," said Jenny. "Do you know a bit about alchemy?"

"Only that it's about turning lead into gold," admitted Sam.

"Well, that's the simple version, deary, but there's a lot more to alchemy than that. It was named after Egypt, you know."

"Seriously?"

"Oh yes. Chem is the ancient name of Egypt, hence the name Al-Chem-y. The Secret Fire is another name for it. Now, what does that other symbol stand for . . . ? I know the symbol for gold is the sun, but what is the circle with an arrow?" She paused for a moment. "Oh, I know! Iron! It stands for iron." Jenny seemed very pleased with herself. "So, maybe this map does show the old channel and the location of the barge."

Or the Panehesy, Sam thought. He didn't think his uncle had come all the way to Al Minya to search for an old barge. His rough map now had far more meaning, but not quite enough. He pointed to the iron symbol. "Is there any way of knowing where this is?"

Jenny flicked through a few more pages. "I'm afraid not, dear. The only other entry refers to the decision not to recover the barge. But all it says here is it was a few miles upstream. I guess they had other things to worry about at the time."

"A few miles," said Sam despondently. "You could search for weeks, months even, and never get close to finding it."

"Unless . . . ," said Jenny.

"Unless what?"

"If your drawing is a good copy, you could match it up with an actual map of the Nile. And I know the perfect book. It has aerial shots of the river up and downstream of Al Minya."

"That's great," said Sam. "Can I see it?"

Jenny laughed at Sam's excitement. "Well, that's the funny thing. It was your professor who asked if I happened to have a book like that. I wasn't sure, to be honest," she said, motioning to the crowded book-shelves behind her. "As you can imagine, it took me a while to find it, but when I did, I sent it over to the professor's motel. That was last Friday. It's a big old thing, quite expensive, but he assured me he would take good care of it."

A big book. That was the kind of thing you would have to clear a whole table to make room for. Sam knew he needed to get back to the motel, but before he could come up with a polite way to make his exit, a buzzer went off.

"Well, would you look at that," said Jenny, pointing at a small black-and-white monitor on the floor beside her. "It appears I have another male visitor. When it rains, it pours, eh, deary?"

Sam hadn't noticed the security camera above the front door of the museum when he'd arrived, but the new visitor had. The black-and-white picture made him look bald, but Sam knew in real life he had very short blond hair. Sam also knew he had just seconds to come up with an escape plan.

"Jenny, I don't suppose there's a back door out of the museum?"

"No, dear, afraid not. But I'm popping down to greet my new arrival, so it's no problem to let you out the front." Jenny noticed Sam still staring at the monitor. "Do you know that gentleman?"

"Kind of."

"You don't look very pleased to see him."

Sam shrugged, unsure about how much he should let on. He needn't have worried. Jenny didn't need an explanation.

"Well, that's that, then," she said, getting to her feet. "I'll tell him you're not here."

Sam watched the man fidgeting impatiently on the monitor. "I've got a better idea. Can you tell him I'm in the bathroom?"

"Are you sure? I'm quite happy to send him on his way."

"No, that's fine," Sam assured her.

"Suit yourself," Jenny called out, heading for the stairs. "The bathrooms are just down the corridor."

Sam was already running to them.

"WHERE IS HE?" THE MAN DEMANDED AS he reached the second floor.

"I told you," Jenny called out from halfway up the stairs. "The bathroom."

"Which way?"

The sound of thumping boots told Sam the man had spotted the sign.

One hard kick sent the bathroom door slamming back against the tiled wall. It was a small bathroom, with an old, cracked urinal and three narrow cubicles. The doors of two were open. The middle one was shut, and just visible, in the gap between the bottom of the door and the floor, were the tips of Sam's sneakers.

"Hello again, Sam. You are busy, yes? No problem. I will wait."

The man leaned back against the wall, breathing heavily after his stair-running and door-kicking heroics.

From his hiding place under Jenny's desk, Sam

knew it was time to make his move. It wouldn't be long before the Short-Haired Man discovered he was waiting on an empty pair of shoes. Sam took off down the stairs, mouthing a hurried *thank you* to the stunned museum manager as he passed her. As Sam bolted out the front door, an angry scream from the second-floor bathroom told him the ruse was up. He'd known Jenny wouldn't be able to get rid of the man, but the bathroom deception was all he could come up with. It had meant losing his shoes, but at least he'd gotten away.

A few minutes later the decision to sacrifice his shoes didn't feel like such a smart move. The midday sun had baked the footpath crazily hot. Sam felt blisters forming on his feet with every step. Ignoring the pain, he kept up his pace. He had to get back to the motel. There was no way of knowing if the Short-Haired Man knew about the Nefertiti, but he had no choice. The book was there, so now it was a race against time to get back to the motel and get his hands on it.

And he would. Just not the way he expected.

15
WHERE THERE'S SMOKE

NOW IT WAS SAM'S TURN TO KICK DOWN a door. At least he would have tried if he hadn't been so exhausted. By the time he got to the motel, weeping blisters had formed on both feet. What hit him as he entered the reception area was how good it felt standing on the cool stone tiles.

The second thing that entered his mind was the feeling there was someone behind him.

Sitting in a chair behind the door was a man in his thirties who looked like a younger, healthier version of Ahmed. That turned out to be pretty accurate.

"Father, come!" the man yelled, which was what Sam had been about to do.

The plan was to find the book and one of the pairs of shoes he'd spied in his uncle's room and get out, but the look on Ahmed's face when he shuffled out of the back room told Sam things weren't going to work out that way.

Ahmed's eyes lit up as soon as he saw Sam, and he darted back through the doorway with a speed Sam hadn't seen from him before. He returned clutching a fax and muttering a stream of angry-sounding Egyptian. Sam had no idea what he was going on about till he caught a glimpse of his passport photo on the piece of paper.

The Cairo police had finally caught up with him.

The reason for Ahmed's son's presence became clear as two strong hands grabbed Sam from behind and pushed him toward the back room. Ahmed was still jabbering away, but the odd bit of English slipped into his tirade. Sam made out the words "police," "uncle," and "bad man."

He was guided firmly through the small back office and into a small storeroom. Rows of wooden shelves lined each wall, crammed with old computers, crockery, and other assorted pieces of junk. But what caught

Sam's attention was sitting near the door at eye level—an oversized book. The title, embossed in gold, proudly proclaimed *Nile Aerial Survey*.

Ahmed's son let go of Sam. He looked relieved with how smoothly things had gone and offered a translation by way of thanks. "My father is very upset with you and your uncle," he said, though not unkindly. "He received fax from police saying you are both in trouble. He is calling them now. . . . I don't think you will be here long."

Sam smiled and nodded as Ahmed's son locked the door. He was probably thinking it was strange that the young criminal didn't appear more upset, but at that moment Sam just wanted to be left alone with the book.

When Jenny had told him the book was big, the empty table in Jasper's room suddenly made sense. That's where the book had been. But Jasper hadn't taken it into the desert, so he'd made a copy of the map and left one under the bed for backup. And now Sam knew that the table had been empty because Ahmed and his wife had been worried about Jasper doing a runner, and they'd swiped the book as an insurance policy.

Sam didn't have to search through the book for long. His uncle had marked the page with a business card for a local company. When Sam laid the hand-drawn map over the image in the book, it matched perfectly.

Sam quickly copied the coordinates for the location of the *Panehesy* from the original map. He decided he would try to get the book back to Jenny if he managed to get himself out of this mess, which brought him back to this most recent dilemma: locked in a room, with the police on the way.

There were only two ways out. The door, which a quick investigation showed wouldn't have been out of place in a jail, and a window, which was too high and too small, on the back wall. If Ahmed's son had been in the storeroom at that moment, he would have seen the look he'd been expecting, because Sam had worked out he'd have to be a magician to get out of there.

AFTER THUMPING THE DOOR TO GET AHMED'S attention, he'd tried to talk his way out. The motel owner turned jailer made it clear that the magic words he wanted to hear were *I have money*, and Sam had none. But in the middle of trying to come up with a second plan of possible escape, another problem proved to be a last-second solution to a dilemma he hadn't anticipated.

The Short-Haired Man's arrival at the museum had prevented Sam from making a proper trip to the bathroom, and stuck there in the Nefertiti Motel's holding cell, things had started to get desperate. Until Sam had found two empty glass jars on one of the wooden shelves.

They were now full glass jars, and Sam had thoughtfully placed them near the door, for easy disposal.

Then they started to give off smoke.

Sam wondered if he'd damaged himself by holding on for so long, but as his view of the jars of golden liquid became hazy, he realized that the situation was far more serious than that. The smoke wasn't coming from his pee. It was coming from behind the jars, through the gap under the door.

A high-pitched scream punctuated Sam's revelation, and it spurred him into action. As he banged on the door, he could hear Ahmed's wife talking frantically in the other room.

"Hey! What's going on?" Sam yelled. It was bad timing, because at that moment the fire alarm went off and clanging bells drowned out his cries. More banging failed to bring anyone, and Sam began to suspect that Ahmed and his wife had done a runner of their own.

The door didn't feel hot or even warm, and as Sam continued banging on the door, he searched his mind for remnants of the talk the local fireman had given at his school. Stop, drop, and roll? No need for that. Not yet. But more and more smoke was coming in under the door. Sam began to feel dizzy as the smoke wafted up around his head, and the fireman's grim proclamation came back to him: *"Smoke is the number one killer."*

A stack of nasty-looking Mighty Nefertiti tea towels sat on one of the shelves. Soaked in water they would do a decent job of holding back the deadly white mist seeping in under the door. There was no water, but there was liquid. Two jars' full.

Sam moved to the back wall of the storeroom. The pee-soaked tea towels performed just like the fireman had said they would, but maybe it was already too late. He slumped to the floor, fighting to stay conscious in the smoke-filled room. The sound of splintering wood echoed through the small space. Sam looked up, but his vision was obscured by the clouds of thick white smoke bellowing in through the hole where the door had been. A beam of light sliced through the haze. The last thing Sam saw before he passed out was a bright yellow giant appearing out of the smoke.

16

WAKEY-WAKEY

"I'M SORRY ABOUT ALL THIS, SAM. REALLY."

The words reached Sam before he was completely awake. As he came to, he had no idea where he was, but visions of the last few moments in the storeroom flooded back into his mind and he bolted upright.

Mary, hovering over the bed, had no time to get out of the way. Their heads met with a meaty *thud*. Sam didn't feel a thing, but the impact sent Mary reeling back across the room.

The door burst open, and Bassem filled the frame, his eyes darting from Sam to Mary.

"It's okay, Bassem," Mary reassured him. "Everything's okay." He didn't seem convinced and left the door ajar after backing out. Through the gap Sam caught a glimpse of the bright yellow rubber boots he was wearing. He glared at Mary.

"Everything is far from okay," he hissed. "What just happened? Who are you?"

Mary, still groggy from the knock on the head, wasn't feeling quite as apologetic now. "What happened? Well, let's see. . . . We saved you from the police. How about that?"

"By nearly killing me?"

"We didn't nearly kill you . . . but we might have overdone it a bit on the sleeping gas," she confessed.

"Sleeping gas?"

"That was Bassem's idea. Knock out the motel owners and break you out of the storeroom."

"How did you even know I was there?"

"Bassem has a contact with the local police," said Mary. "As soon as the motel owner reported you, we knew about it."

Sam took his first proper look around the small room. "Where are we exactly?

"A safe house that Bassem organized."

"Okay. So, next question, and most important . . . who are you?"

"My name is Mary Verulam."

"Verulam?" Sam remembered the letter he'd found

at his uncle's apartment. "The Verulam Corporation pays my school fees."

"I know. Look, Sam, your uncle was working for my father. He's worried about him."

"You've been watching me to see if I lead you to my uncle. I heard you on the phone at the helicopter."

"Yes . . . and no," Mary stammered. "I didn't lie to you. I want to help you. You heard me talking to my father. I wanted permission to tell you the whole story."

"So? What is the whole story, then?"

"I don't know exactly."

Sam rolled his eyes.

"I'm being straight with you, Sam. Your uncle was following a lead my father gave him. That *Panehesy* clue you found in Jasper's apartment came from him."

Sam opened his mouth to speak, but broke into a violent coughing fit. Mary picked up the jug on the bedside table and poured Sam a glass of water, which he drank greedily. It helped wash the burnt taste out of his mouth, which he guessed had been caused by the sleeping gas, or smoke, or whatever he'd been knocked out with.

"I am really sorry, Sam," Mary repeated. "Bassem didn't think the gas would reach you, but he said you had tried to block it out with wet rags. Smart move."

Sam smiled as he thought of the soggy Nefertiti

tea towels. He wondered if Ahmed would still try to sell them.

"We needed to rescue you in a hurry," continued Mary, "and it was all we could come up with."

"Yeah, but sleeping gas?" Sam took another sip of water, savoring the way it soothed his stinging throat. "Where did you get it?"

"Bassem likes to be prepared," said Mary.

"Obviously." Sam stared at the glass in his hand as he tried to process everything Mary had told him. He could feel her eyes on him. His head was spinning and his throat felt like it had been rubbed with sandpaper. "So, what now?"

"You tell me," said Mary. "We are here to help you."

"You mean, you want to know where my uncle is."

Mary looked frustrated, but it didn't show when she spoke. "Yes, Sam, we want to find your uncle. I know you don't believe me yet, but we are on the same side."

The room fell silent. Sam took another sip of water. Could he trust her and the Egyptian giant? They had saved him, twice. "There are other people looking for my uncle, and the *Panehesy*. Two men were after me in Cairo. One of them is here in Al Minya."

Mary nodded. "Even more reason for you to let us help. Do you know where your uncle is?"

Sam wasn't prepared to play all his cards just yet. "I think so," he said.

"And you think he's located the *Panehesy*?"

Sam nodded.

"Okay. Well, you don't have to say where. Just tell me what you need from us."

Sam knew exactly what he needed. The same thing his uncle had used to get to the *Panehesy*. The clue had been the business card in the map book: AL MINYA 4X4 RENTALS. "I need transport into the desert," said Sam. "Can you organize that?"

Mary nodded. "No problem. Bassem—"

Sam cut her off. "Let me guess. Bassem knows a guy."

IT TURNED OUT THAT HE KNEW A COUPLE of guys.

Bassem was out when the first one arrived. As Sam followed Mary downstairs to open the door, he checked out the safe house. The place was clean and modern, with brown floor tiles and off-white walls, but it was obvious no one lived there permanently. Most of the rooms were empty, and there were no signs of any personal items on the shelves or walls.

The man at the door was holding a large cardboard box. He walked in, dropped it in the hallway, and left without saying a word.

"You can tell he's a friend of Bassem's," Sam said as Mary opened the box.

It was full of camping equipment. Clearly, Mary had been expecting it, because she pulled out a pair of military-issue desert boots and a lightweight brown jacket. "Here you go," she said, tossing them to Sam. "You're going to need these. I hope the boots fit. I measured while you were asleep."

Sam looked at his bandaged feet. "Guess I should say thanks for this, too."

A rumbling sound filled the hallway as the roller door in the garage opened. Sam and Mary entered as Bassem rolled in on an ultramodern quad bike, the kind ridden by endurance riders. Sam had seen them in magazines. This bike was painted in a flat desert brown color and had four spotlights mounted on the front. Bassem skidded to a stop on the polished concrete floor as another identical quad rolled in behind. The second rider left without saying a word. Sam was beginning to think the silent giant and his friends communicated telepathically.

Bassem got to work sorting the camping equipment into two loads for the bikes.

"So, what exactly is my uncle doing for your father?" asked Sam. He still wasn't prepared to share everything he knew, but that wasn't going to stop him from tapping Mary for more info.

"Pyramids," she replied. "I guess you could say they're a bit of a family obsession."

Sam was confused. "I thought this was about alchemy. You know, the Secret Fire." He threw that factoid in to show Mary he was clued up on the subject, even though his knowledge stretched back less than twenty-four hours.

"Secret Fire? That's interesting," said Mary. "Did you know that some scholars speculate that 'pyramid' means 'the fire within'? There could be a link there."

"Could be? You mean you don't know?"

"Not really," Mary admitted. "Look, my father has kept me in the dark about his research for most of my life." She glanced at Bassem, who was still busy with the bikes. "He always said it was for my own protection."

"So, what changed?" asked Sam. "How come you're here?"

"I was supposed to keep an eye on your situation from Cairo. Father only agreed to that because Bassem was with me. But then I persuaded him we needed to come and help you."

"So, we've got pyramids and alchemy. But how does Akhenaten fit in? Unless . . ."

"Unless what?"

Sam thought back to his chat with Jenny. "The alchemy symbol for gold is the sun, and that was Akhenaten's thing, right?"

"That's right," said Mary. "He banned all gods and made everyone worship the sun in Amarna."

Sam nodded. "So maybe he took something to Amarna. Something from the pyramids. Something to do with alchemy."

"My grandfather always thought the pyramids at Giza were empty shells," said Mary. "I read it in one of the research papers he wrote when he was a student."

"Your grandfather?"

"I told you this stuff was a family obsession. Jason Verulam was an Egyptologist before World War Two."

"Did he die?"

"Yes, but not in the war. Although he might as well have. He came home from Egypt in some kind of shock and spent seventy-three years in a hospital bed, in a catatonic state. He only died this year."

"Cata-*what*?"

"He was a vegetable. Couldn't talk, move. It was like he was dead."

"Sorry," said Sam. "I know what it's like to lose family."

"No, Sam, it's nothing like you losing your parents. I hardly knew my granddad. I didn't know him at all, really. He was always just a body on the bed for me. But you know what's interesting? After he died, my father found a key to a safe-deposit box, and the next day he got in touch with your uncle. I think my grand-father knew about the *Panehesy*."

The conversation ended as Bassem signaled it was time to go by starting his bike and opening the garage door.

Mary grabbed one of the helmets on the second bike. "Come on," she said, tossing it to Sam. "You're riding with me."

"And how come you get to drive?"

"You can have a go next time," said Mary, strapping on her helmet.

"Oh sure, next time we're in the desert looking for a missing World War Two ship, then I get to drive."

Mary jumped onto the bike and hit the start button. As she revved the engine, she called out, "You'll have to tell us whether we should go upriver or downriver from here."

Sam still didn't want to say too much, but he had to give in a little. "Up," he said.

Mary nodded at Bassem. "Cool. We'll get out of town, and then you can tell us more. If you trust me, that is," she added with a wink.

THE OPPRESSIVE AFTERNOON HEAT HAD driven most people inside, which meant Bassem and Mary mainly had to contend with crazy car and truck drivers and not as many of the human dodge balls that are so common on Egyptian streets.

Sam's previous quad experience totaled one hour in a field on a farm last year. It quickly became obvious from the way Mary handled the bike that she had a lot more practice. Sam wasn't so sure Bassem shared the same confidence in her abilities, because from the moment they left the safe house he kept turning to check on her. It took a while for Sam to work out he was actually checking behind them to make sure they weren't being followed. After that Sam started doing the same thing, but not well enough it turned out, because it was Mary who spotted the tail.

"Don't look, but we're being followed," Mary yelled.

"Does Bassem know?" Sam yelled back.

Up front Bassem appeared to be riding without a care in the world. He'd even dropped his left hand from the handlebar, so his arm was hanging at his side. An unremarkable act that went unnoticed by everyone except Mary and Sam, who saw that one finger of Bassem's left hand was pointing at the intersection just ahead.

"Yep, he knows," said Mary, and when Bassem opened the throttle and tore off up the road, she was right behind him.

Now that the game was on, Sam decided it was okay to turn and get a look at who was behind them: two men in matching black bike leathers on matching black dirt bikes. Their visors were down, so there was no way to know if one of them was the Short-Haired Man, and Sam was happy not to find out.

Bassem and Mary had gotten the jump on the bikers, who lost ground as they struggled to get around a truck full of goats. Sam lost sight of them as Mary took a hard left at the intersection.

They had pulled into a much narrower street with high brick walls lining each side. Bassem dismounted near the corner while Mary rode on a little farther before stopping. Then she and Sam turned to watch. This was where Mary's minder had decided to make his stand, but Sam couldn't work out how. Then the answer came when Bassem slid a long, telescopic steel rod out of the left arm of his leather jacket. The guy really did come prepared for anything.

The two bikes came around the corner single file. Bassem took one step back and flicked the rod up like a samurai presenting his sword to his opponent. As the first bike came toward him, he swung down and across in one smooth, vicious motion that caught the rider in the middle of his chest. He might as well have ridden into a brick wall.

As he flew backward and crashed onto the foot-path, his bike rolled on as if it were happy to be free of its rider. The joy didn't last long, however; the front wheel hit a gutter, and the bike somersaulted through the air like a mechanical dolphin, but without a graceful landing. Instead, there was the screeching of metal and splintering fiberglass as it hit the wall.

All this happened as the second rider came around the corner. He had only a couple of seconds to avoid a similar fate, but made good use of his time, veering wider than his mate and ducking to avoid the lethal sting of Bassem's telescopic sword.

Having avoided certain injury, the rider raced on toward Mary and Sam, but the loss of his companion had left him with odds he didn't like, and he sped on down the lane and disappeared around the next bend.

Bassem mounted his quad and motioned for Mary to do the same on hers.

"That was incredible," said Sam as they cruised past the first rider sprawled out on the footpath. When they pulled up alongside Bassem, Sam intended to say something to the guy, but before he could, Bassem handed him two small apple-sized metal balls and took off down the main street.

"Grenades!? Why did he give me these?" asked Sam as Mary followed Bassem.

"Because he doesn't think it's over yet."

17

HOT PURSUIT

BASSEM INCREASED THE PACE, AND AS THEY raced through the streets, tantalizing glimpses of the Nile flashed between the buildings up ahead. Despite their speed Sam could feel the sun baking him through his jacket, but it wasn't as intense as when they'd first left the safe house. But the drop in temperature had also brought the human dodge balls back out in force.

It was one of the crazy things Sam noticed in Cairo, and it appeared to be just as big in Al Minya: the endless supply of people prepared to throw their lives into the hands of others by making mad dashes across lanes full of speeding traffic. Perhaps it was the heat that made them want to get from A to B as fast as possible, and perhaps it was also the heat that fried any kind of sense out of them, because the majority of these street runners wouldn't even wait for a decent gap in the traffic—they just ran. Sometimes they ran in groups, which at least made them easier to spot, but the really dangerous ones were the solo runners who could dart out into your lane from behind a truck at any time. For someone behind a wheel or handlebars it was either a fun way to test your reaction time or a nerve-fraying horror ride, depending on your state of mind. Mary dealt with Al Minya's dodge balls well, but Sam was certain his role as backseat spotter was helping her along. He got so caught up in it that he stopped checking behind them. Luckily, Bassem hadn't.

They were on a wide road running parallel with the Nile when Sam noticed they were reaching the outskirts of town. The buildings started getting shorter and dirtier. Human bowling pins were still taking their chances, but there weren't as many. Soon they were passing small herds of goats and donkeys. Sam had seen the same thing in Cairo plenty of times, but the farther along the road they went, the more livestock they encountered. Then Sam saw why. They had arrived at the Al Minya Stock Market. Perhaps they weren't heading out into the desert on the quads after all, he thought. Maybe Bassem was planning on taking them old school, on horses or camels, because Sam couldn't see another reason for bringing them here.

Mary followed her minder across a parking lot that had been converted into a massive animal pen. Small herds of goats and donkeys had been roped off into separate blocks, each one tended by a sun-ravaged man. They navigated their way down the narrow aisles, between the live produce.

Bassem's destination was a battered old truck loaded with goats. The bikes swung around behind it, and Sam assumed they were going to get off, but Bassem didn't. Instead, he leaned across the handlebars and peered between the wooden slats as if he were inspecting the goats. Mary copied him, and Sam, not wanting to be the odd one out, did the same. It was only then that he saw Bassem had brought them to the perfect spot to view the market undetected. They hadn't come to dump the bikes; they'd come to dump their tail.

Right on cue one of the black-clad bikers rode in through the gate. It had to be the second guy. He rolled slowly into the market, scanning the crowded square. Sitting there in full leathers on his slick dirt bike, he looked completely out of place. Sam couldn't work out why the lone biker wasn't attracting more stares from the old men scattered among the stock, but then it occurred to him this market had been here for hundreds of years. They'd probably seen it all.

The rider moved farther into the square, using his legs to roll the bike forward as he twisted his head left and right, searching for his prey. It seemed obvious to Sam that the guy was about to give up, and if he rode on, it would bring him straight to their hiding place. Why were they just sitting there watching? Shouldn't they be getting clear of the place? Sam turned to ask Bassem what he had in mind, but he didn't have to. The answer was in his hands: two hand grenades, like the ones he had given Sam.

"You can't do that!" protested Sam in a whisper, but it was too late. As he spoke, Bassem pulled the pins and lobbed the two green balls up and over the top of the truck.

"Throw yours," demanded Mary, but Sam had his eyes shut and his hands over his ears, ready for the blast. Mary dug her hands into Sam's pockets, fished out his grenades, and repeated Bassem's action. By the time they landed, the first two had already gone off, and chaos had exploded in the square.

High-pitched shrieks from goats, donkeys, and men combined. It was like a bomb going off on Noah's Ark. A *smoke* bomb. Four of them. Sam opened his eyes, peered through the wooden slats, and caught a brief glimpse of the clouds of thick white and green smoke billowing into the air, and then all trace of the market was gone with only the earsplitting noise to tell the story.

Mary started her quad, and they moved off behind Bassem, sticking close because the drifting smoke had cut visibility down to a few feet. A family of stamped-ing goats charged for the same alleyway the quads were heading for, but they were the lucky few. Back at ground zero it was a densely packed mass of men and animals, and trapped in the middle of them was a very pissed off guy on a dirt bike.

The alley they were in ran the length of the market. As they got farther from the square, the smoke melted away and the cries and bleats faded. The end of the alley was the end of the market, and after that was just the desert. That's where Bassem was leading them.

Mary gunned the quad as they hit the first sand dune. She guided the machine up the slope like an expert. As they crested the first rise, Bassem was already halfway down the other side. Mary took this as a challenge, squeezing more power out of the bike. She slotted into Bassem's tracks and raced down the hill after him. Eager not to give the impression that the speed was freaking him out, Sam hadn't been holding Mary too tightly, but now his instinct for self-preservation over-ruled his ego, and he gripped her a little firmer around the waist. By the third dune he was more relaxed and really starting to enjoy the ride.

THEY WERE RIDING A TAN-COLORED OCEAN with peaks and troughs of sand worn smooth by the wind. Sam had always wanted to ride quads in the desert, but it never quite happened. There was always a museum to see or a boring dig to help out on.

That was the thing about his vacations in Egypt: They felt like an extension of school. Jasper had always acted more like a teacher than family, and that hurt. In the background, Sam always had the nagging feeling that his uncle hadn't really wanted to take on the role of guardian.

Sam pushed those thoughts from his mind. None of them mattered now. His uncle was in trouble, and time was running out. He had to find Jasper fast.

That's when he began to worry about the direction they were going. Sam hadn't told Mary the exact location of the *Panehesy*, only that it was upriver, but now they were heading *away* from the Nile. Sam decided to stay silent. Mary and Bassem hadn't let him down yet, so there had to be a reason they were going this way.

Then they reached the top of another dune, and in the distance Sam saw a small oasis shimmering in the afternoon sun.

FROM THE TOP OF EACH DUNE THE OASIS
got a little closer and a little bigger, and then it was in
front of them, at the bottom of a long, gentle slope. It
wasn't much to look at—just five or six tennis courts'
worth of palm trees jammed together. Bassem led them
halfway around the edge until he found a gap in the
greenery they could fit the bikes through.

They weaved slowly through the dense foliage, heading, Sam assumed, for the well that would be located
somewhere near the center. But Bassem seemed to have
something else in mind, and he suddenly killed the
engine and dismounted. Mary did the same thing as the
big man fished a pair of binoculars out of the bag tied to
his quad and started walking back along the path they
had just made.

"I think Bassem's worried we're still being followed,"
said Mary as she watched him go.

"There's no way that guy on the bike got free in
time to follow us, is there?" asked Sam.

"I don't think so, but I've learned to trust Bassem's
instincts. He knows his stuff."

"He knows a lot of stuff," said Sam, thinking back
to the samurai stunt in town. "Where did you find that
guy?"

"He's kind of an old family friend," she said. "He's had

an interesting life. He might tell you about it sometime."

"I doubt it," said Sam

"What do you mean?"

"Well, that would require Bassem to actually speak, wouldn't it?"

Mary laughed. "Yeah, you're right. The big guy's never really been much of a talker, but we seem to get by."

Sam and Mary followed the newly made path till they saw Bassem near the point where they'd entered the oasis. He was tucked behind a fallen palm tree, scanning the horizon through the binoculars. Sam and Mary didn't join him, opting instead for the shade a little farther back.

Bassem watched, and Sam and Mary watched him watching, but there wasn't much to see. The Egyptian was as still as the dead trunk he was leaning on. Minutes ticked by, and the sitting and doing nothing began to get on Sam's nerves. It had been a crazy few days. He had done more and slept less than he had ever thought possible, and it felt like he was on the homestretch, but instead of a sprint to the finish line he was stuck in a dinky little oasis doing nothing! Why not just keep going? The desert was a big place; surely they could outrun anyone who was behind them? *If* they were still being followed. And it was a big *if*. Just like it was a big desert.

Despite his frustration Sam wasn't going to start questioning Bassem. So, they sat, watched, and waited. And to take his mind off the waiting, Sam tried to learn more about Mary's family obsession with pyramids.

"You said your grandfather thought the pyramids at Giza were empty shells. I thought they were for burying the pharaohs in?"

"That's what they teach you in school," said Mary, "but it doesn't always add up. No pharaohs were ever found in the pyramids at Giza. In fact, in the whole of Egypt only one pyramid has ever been found that was being used as burial tomb."

"So what about the King's Chamber in the big pyramid? Wasn't that where the pharaoh was supposed to be buried?"

"Wow, I'm impressed! You do know a bit about Egypt after all. Thought it bored you to tears?"

"Yeah, well, I guess if you get hit over the head with the stuff enough times, a bit sinks in," said Sam. "So what's the King's Chamber?"

"The King's and Queen's Chambers were only given those names in the sixth century. The sarcophagus looks like a coffin, but, like I said, no mummy was ever found in there. There aren't even any hieroglyphics inside the chamber. How do you explain that for a place that was supposed to be the burial site of the great Khufu? He was the pharaoh they say built the Great Pyramid at Giza," she added.

Sam rolled his eyes. "I also know that. I'm not a complete ignoramus when it comes to Egyptology. I just find it a bit boring."

"Not so boring now, is it?"

Mary was right. This week had been light-years from anything resembling boring. Sam hoped he would look back on the whole thing as a great adventure. But right there, at that moment, he just wanted it over and done with and his uncle safe.

"Remind me what the sarcophagus looks like again?" he asked.

"Give me your sketchbook, and I'll draw it for you. What? You think you're the only one who can draw?" asked Mary in response to Sam's raised eyebrows.

"It was carved out of a solid block of red granite," Mary said as she drew. "Two-point-five cubits by one-point-five cubits by one-point-five cubits. Too small to fit a body."

"What's a cubit?" asked Sam.

"About twenty-one inches. It was the Egyptian measurement system."

"Not bad," said Sam, admiring Mary's pencil work. "So what was it built for?"

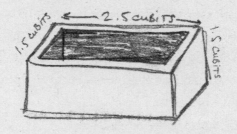

"That, my young Egyptologist," said Mary, adopting the voice of an elderly university professor, "is the sixty-four-thousand-dollar question." Mary stopped as the sound of rustling leaves drew their attention back to Bassem.

The big man was on the move. As he came back toward them, Sam saw a flicker of movement over his shoulder. Up on the ridge the man on the dirt bike was watching the oasis. Sam's mouth fell open in surprise as Bassem glided past. Mary had to grab Sam by his jacket and haul him to his feet. But it wasn't the reappearance of the two-wheeled stalker that had stunned him. It was that he had just heard the first ever words from Bassem's mouth.

"You need to take off your clothes. Fast."

18

DUMMY RUN

IT SEEMED LIKE THOSE FIRST FEW WORDS had opened the floodgates. Mary caught up to Bassem as they headed back to the quads, and he talked all the way. Sam couldn't quite make out what they were saying, but he assumed it was to do with him getting his gear off.

"You really do have to get undressed, Sam," Mary urged when they got to the bikes. Behind her, Bassem began pulling the carefully packed camping equipment and water bottles off the bikes and dumping it in a pile on the ground. When the giant Egyptian turned and saw Sam still standing there fully clothed, he locked his dark, brooding eyes on him. For a man who didn't talk much, his look spoke volumes. Sam scuttled behind a palm to disrobe.

"What's this all about?" he said, trying not to sound pissed off, although he figured he kind of had the right to be.

Sam needn't have been worried about Mary trying to sneak a peek. She was busy on her hands and knees collecting dead palm leaves. "Those guys following us might have some high-tech help," she said as she worked.

"What do you mean?" asked Sam.

"Bassem thinks they might have been tracking us on a spy satellite. He reckons that's the only way they could have found us out here."

"Spy satellite? But why does that mean I have to get my gear off?" Sam asked as he tossed his jeans, shirt, and jacket around the tree.

"Don't worry. We're not going to leave you here naked," said Mary

Sam looked down as another pile of clothes was tossed back to him. "Hang on! What? Leave me? I thought you said you were going to help."

"Get dressed and I'll explain," said Mary.

Sam didn't need to be told twice, and when he

stepped out from behind his modesty screen, he saw Mary working on Bassem's plan.

"If we are being watched by a spy satellite, Bassem says you're going to have to walk from here, Sam." She looked up from her work. "Sorry. I wanted to come with you, but the big guy won't let me, and it would kind of ruin his plan anyway."

"That's cool." Sam was lying. It didn't feel cool at all. For a start, he didn't know where to walk because he had no idea where he was.

"Hey." Another word passed Bassem's lips, and this came with a gift as he tossed an oversized mobile phone to Sam.

"There's a GPS unit in that phone," said Mary, raking up more dead palm fronds with her hands. "You've got the coordinates of the *Panehesy*, yeah?"

Sam held up the hand-drawn map.

"Good," said Mary. "Program them in, and that thing will lead you right there."

"Okay." Sam was saying okay, but he wasn't thinking it. Instead, he was thinking of a couple of very un-okay things, but then Mary piped up again and cut them off.

"You find the *Panehesy* while we lose this guy once and for all. Then we'll get the chopper and come find you." Mary pointed to the GPS. "Keep that switched on. As long as there's a signal, it will lead us right to you."

"Okay." There were still a couple of un-okays banging around in Sam's skull, but Mary's building project was finished and Bassem was revving his bike impatiently.

Sam helped Mary load her new creation onto her bike.

"Thanks, Sam. See you soon."

Sam said "okay" one more time, but it was drowned out by the noise of Mary racing off after Bassem.

THE TWO QUADS BURST OUT OF THE OASIS slightly farther around from the point they had entered, but not too far. It was important that the man on the ridge saw the breakout. And what exactly did he see? His targets, spooked from their hiding place and making another run for it. The dangerous Egyptian in front. The girl following closely with the boy.

That was exactly what Bassem had been counting on. If the man hadn't been in such a rush to follow the fleeing quads, he might have used his binoculars, and then he might have noticed that Sam had suddenly lost a lot of weight. Mary hadn't had time to collect enough palm leaves to stuff the clothes, but fake Sam was light and that meant Mary could ring more speed out of her bike. The pace would eventually take its toll on fake Sam, and after a few miles his head would fall off, but by then the real Sam would be long gone.

The dirt bike rider took the easiest path, along the ridge, until he linked up with the tracks left by Bassem and Mary. From the shadows on the edge of the oasis Sam watched him drop down off the top of the dune and disappear from sight. He had no idea where Bassem was leading the man or how he planned to lose him, but he knew where he needed to go: exactly three miles due west.

Sam didn't think the journey would be too tough, but he quickly discovered that trekking across sand on foot was far harder than gliding over dunes on a quad. The first couple of miles were just hard going. Sam made frequent stops to drink from the bottle in the backpack Mary had left him and to check the GPS. Not because he was worried about heading the wrong way, but because it also told him how far he had to go.

It was the last three quarters of a mile when things got really grim. Five days with little sleep and no proper food had taken their toll. Sam felt like he'd run a marathon, then been forced to go around again. The dunes seemed to grow bigger, Sam got slower, and the "distance to destination" readout hardly moved between breaks.

Luckily, the heat was easing as the sun's long arc across the sky came to an end. It was an impressive sight. A flaming golden disc hovering in the deep blue afternoon sky.

Seeing it like this, Sam could understand how the inhabitants of this harsh land had gotten so obsessed with it. Akhenaten translated as "the horizon of Aten" and now, as the day waned, that was his destination. It would be dark soon, and while there was also a flashlight in the bag, nightfall would make his search harder. But search for what? The question burned as bright as Aten. He didn't expect to find a rusting ship sticking out of the desert, or his uncle sitting on a campstool sipping a mug of sweet tea. That would have been too easy. He only hoped that he would know what he was meant to be looking for when he got there. And so he pushed on, dune after dune, toward the horizon of Aten.

ACCORDING TO THE GPS IT WAS THE HOME-stretch. The last tenth of a mile. The dunes began to shrink, the going got easier, and Sam's rising expectations gave him a new burst of energy. His second wind. Wasn't that what runners called it? Sam figured he was onto his third or fourth.

Finally, he reached the top of a small dune, and ahead

was the Nile, stretched out like a glistening blue ribbon, framed top and bottom with the green bands of vegetation that fed off the life-giving waters. But not in front of Sam. Here the desert ran all the way down to the river's edge, and as he surveyed the scene, he knew he was lost.

It wasn't that he didn't know where he was. The GPS told him that just ahead was the area that was once part of the Nile but had been swallowed up in the storm of '42. It shouldn't have come as a surprise to Sam that the area was much bigger than it had appeared on the map, but it was huge—a massive expanse of undulating desert spoiled only by a few small depressions. But it took only a second to see that the area was empty. He hadn't expected to see a ship sticking out of the sand, but he had hoped for *something*. Some sign of his uncle. But there was nothing. Sam had no idea what to do next, so he sat and watched Aten's departure.

IN THE LAST FEW MINUTES OF DAYLIGHT, as the sun dropped beneath the horizon, the shallow dips in the sand began to fill with shadows. From Sam's front-row seat at the top of the rise, the landscape looked as if it were dotted with giant bowls of weak tea. Each dip created a slightly different oval shape of darkness, but one looked out of place. In one depression the curved line of the shadow was spoiled by something lumpy.

Sam stood up, trying to suppress his hope while also watching carefully.

As the last useful rays of sunlight played across the sand, Sam walked toward the dip. As he got closer, he started walking more quickly, his heart beating faster. During daylight hours it would have been impossible to spot, because the camouflage netting blended perfectly with the color of the sand. But now, with the shadows, the color differences were clear.

Sam was boiling hot, but not from the jog. He was thinking about that game little kids play where someone hides something and they tell you how close you are to it—warm . . . warmer . . . getting warmer . . . hot.

And Sam was boiling hot.

19
THE MEASURE
OF A PLAN

SAM HAD TO STAY BENT OVER TO STOP HIS
hair from getting caught in the camouflage netting as
he looked around Jasper's tiny campsite. A folding table
and quad bike took up most of the floor space. The
faded orange paint was peeling off the machine, but
the words on the tank were still readable: AL MINYA
4X4 RENTALS. Small holes had been dug into the walls
for storage, perhaps for a candle and radio, though
everything was gone now. Only the table and bike
had been left behind, or so Sam thought until he
shined his flashlight under the table.

The item was half buried in the sand and looked as

though Jasper had used it for a footrest. Had it been too big to carry or simply not needed anymore? Sam pulled EEF's missing metal detector from the desert's sandy grip; the thick metal shaft was warm after a day baking in Jasper's pit. The small canvas find bag, where the operator would place anything found while out scanning the sand, dangled from the handgrip. From the way it swayed in the evening breeze, it seemed empty, but Sam opened the pouch anyway. He hadn't gotten this far without learning to check everything closely. And this time his instincts paid off. Tucked in the bottom of the bag, and barely visible, was a folded piece of paper, which Sam opened immediately and used his flashlight to read closely.

Saturday, July 18

Dear Jasper,

I am thrilled you have decided to accept my offer. Enclosed with this letter is the only clue I can offer you. Panehesy, as you may know, was a high priest of the Pharaoh Akhenaten, but it was also a ship that entered the Nile in 1942. I only recently came into possession of this information. I know it's not much, but I am sure a man with your background will be able to make the most of it.

Jasper, I realize your motivation for taking on this assignment is strictly personal, but trust me when I tell you that there is far more at stake than you can possibly imagine. You are on the trail of one of Egypt's greatest missing treasures. The importance of this endeavor cannot be underestimated; neither can the people who oppose it. I don't wish to cause you undue concern, but I would advise you to keep the details to yourself.

I look forward to your success and the opportunity to meet you in person, at which point I will be more than happy to share with you the full story behind this task you are about to undertake.

Yours sincerely,

Francis Verulam

Sam realized he was looking at the letter that had triggered his whole crazy adventure, and it brought a wry smile to his face to find out that his uncle had been given the "*Panehesy* is a ship from WWII" clue straight out, while he'd had to work it out the hard way. But the letter was only part of the discovery; it was what had been scribbled on the back that got Sam excited. The symbol and doodles would have meant nothing to Sam a few days ago, but knowing what he did now, he realized he had the coded coordinates for the *Panehesy*.

The night had arrived with a vengeance. With no moon the first few stars had the jet-black sky to themselves, but Sam knew many more would follow. Nowhere is the contrast between night and day more exaggerated than in the desert. Unbearable heat gives way to a biting cold that leaves first-time visitors suspecting that they have been teleported to the Arctic.

Away from the polluted glow of the city lights, darkness rules in the desert. As the light from Sam's flashlight crept ahead of him, towering walls of blackness attacked from each side, beating it into a narrow path. Sam didn't care; he needed to see only a few feet in front of him at a time.

There was no question of waiting till dawn. Not when he was so close. With the GPS to track his progress, Sam set out. As he'd figured out from the scribbles on the back of the letter, just 200 feet to the west and 165 feet southwest lay the *Panehesy*.

TEN MINUTES LATER SAM WAS GLAD HE hadn't called Mary to share the news of his discovery. The disappointment had hit him hard and fast as he counted out those last couple of feet. He was standing on a small patch of illuminated sand. It was the spot his uncle had marked, but there was nothing. Just sand. Sam had been so sure when he found the coded coordinates, but that confidence evaporated as he'd counted down those last few feet.

Feet. Could that be it? Sam wondered. He was used to thinking in feet, but they used the metric system in Egypt. Could his uncle have jotted the numbers down in meters? The GPS could be set to count in meters. All Sam had to do was backtrack to the campsite and start again.

Seven minutes later Sam was standing on another almost identical-looking patch of sand. Another dead end. A dead end in the dead of night and now, dead tired, Sam collapsed to the sand. He killed the flash-light. No point in wasting the batteries. Not till he worked out what to do next. And right now Sam was all out of ideas.

IT SEEMED LIKE THE UNIVERSE, KNOWING that it didn't have the moon to compete with, had put its entire collection of stars out on display. But the show was wasted on Sam. He was staring straight up, but he didn't see a thing. He was too busy obsessing over how everything had turned out.

Sam had really wanted to believe he had found the *Panehesy* and his uncle, but the empty campsite should have been an obvious clue. Of course it had been abandoned. The *Panehesy* wasn't here, and his uncle had gone. The view he'd first seen from the top of the dune should have been a big hint as well. He'd seen *nothing*. If his uncle had uncovered a ship, there would have had to be some sign of an excavation.

Sam's luck had finally run out. For days he had followed a trail linked by a series of obscure and seemingly unrelated clues. Perhaps the big surprise was that he had gotten this far, but now it seemed the journey was at an end.

But the universe hadn't given up in its attempt to wow its solitary desert audience. It took a massive shooting star to snap Sam out of his self-pitying trance. As the meteor met its match in the outer atmosphere, Sam was forced to acknowledge the stunning view overhead, the million points of flickering light. It always amazed Sam that ancient civilizations like the Egyptians had tried to track and measure their progress.

As he stared, one of his last conversations with Mary drifted back to him. The Egyptians had been obsessed with measurement. In fact, they even created their own: the cubit.

The word hung in Sam's consciousness, dangling on a golden thread like an air freshener from a rearview mirror. Could his uncle's code have had one more layer to it? Mary said a cubit was about twenty-one inches. If the coordinates were in cubits, that would put the magic spot in a totally different location.

The starlight spectacular continued, not at all put off by the fact that their lone desert audience had disappeared. Back at the campsite, Sam set the GPS tracker to the distance in cubits, and for the third time that night he counted off to the southwest.

SIX MINUTES LATER THAT SINKING FEELING hit him again. There were still five cubits to go, but the torchlight told the story. Another identical patch of empty sand. Another dead end. But Sam marched on, determined to count out the last five twenty-one-inch lengths. He had two to go when the sinking feeling began to grow. But now it took on a whole new meaning.

Sam looked down at his feet as they disappeared into the sand. He could feel himself sinking, and as the first fingers of panic took hold, he lifted one foot. Suddenly, the ground beneath him give way completely. A gaping black hole appeared around Sam, and he fell so fast his arms swung above his head, knocking his flashlight out of his hand. Sam's scream faded away as he and his flashlight slipped beneath the surface of the desert.

20

ROTTEN ENTRY

LIKE A HUNGRY BEAST, THE DESERT HAD opened its mouth and swallowed Sam whole, and now he was sliding, feetfirst, down its throat. That thought flashed into Sam's mind, but only as a fleeting interlude from the sheer terror.

The sound track to his hellish slide was the echoey *boom* of his arms hitting the metal sides of the tube he was in. That, and the raspy screeching sound of body and sand scraping across steel. As he lunged for something to grab on to, he tried to make sense of what was happening to him.

Before he could, the ride came to a sudden and painful end. Sam's feet hit hard sand with a jarring impact that made his knees buckle. He immediately took a deep breath, which turned out to be a mistake. His slide under the desert had whipped up a miniature sandstorm. The air was thick with desert dust, and he could still feel it raining down on him like dry snow. Pulling his T-shirt over his mouth, Sam sank to his knees and retrieved his flashlight, which, after a few motivational whacks, buzzed back to life. Sand continued to billow around him. In the light, Sam felt like he was submerged in muddy water at the bottom of a black tube. He rubbed his hand across the curved steel, leaving black powder on his fingers. It was soot.

Sam had wondered how he would get inside the *Panehesy*, but that problem had been solved.

The desert had followed him down the smokestack, but not for the first time. Over the years sand had seeped in through the ship's highest opening. Given time, it would have filled it right up, but that day was still a ways off. Instead of sliding to his death in the engine room, Sam had ended his trip halfway down. The air above was too thick to see far, but he did spot a rope running down from the top. Was it a way out left by someone who had found their way in?

Sam turned his attention to the area around his feet. Wind currents were still kicking up puffs of sand, and that struck Sam as odd, because he couldn't feel a draft coming from above. Dropping to his knees again, Sam took a closer look at the curved steel wall. It wasn't until he ran his hands over the rusting plates that he felt the hole. The blackness on the other side matched the blackness of the soot-covered steel, which made it almost invisible. But now, with the flashlight right next to it, Sam could see that a hole had been cut. And recently. Silvery edges of freshly cut steel flashed like fangs in the flashlight. The *Panehesy* had swallowed Sam, and now it wanted to take a bite. Using his jacket to cover the rough edges, Sam crawled through, into the bowels of the *Panehesy*.

It was the dining room. Three long wooden tables filled the space, with wooden chairs arranged around them. Plates and cutlery were laid out in front of each as if a meal was about to be served. Sam knew he was looking at a moment in time, frozen beneath the desert. The air smelled stale, like the inside of an old leather shoe, and a fine coating of white powder covered every surface. It wasn't the sand Sam had gotten so used to. It was that haunted house stuff—the kind of dust that accumulates magically out of nothing. It gave the room a dull, ghostly finish, and that made the small glint of gold sparkling on the far side of the room even more eye-catching. As Sam got closer, he saw it was a door handle. Decades of accumulated dust had been wiped away in an instant when someone used it.

And now Sam became the second person to go through the door in seventy-three years.

SAM WAS NOW IN A CORRIDOR THAT HAD a row of doors on each side.

At St. Albans all of the boys had to do ballroom dancing, and Sam had been an unwilling victim the year before. It turned out there wasn't just one kind of ballroom dance, but a whole load, and to make it easier to learn them all, their dance teacher had put up posters covered with tiny shoe prints that showed the moves. Sam was reminded of those posters as he viewed what had to be his uncle's footprints in the dust covering the dark wood floor in the hallway.

Jasper had opened the first few doors, and when Sam glanced into them, he saw that each contained two beds, a desk, and a sink. Following the footsteps Sam skipped ahead and went straight to the door at the end of the corridor, just as Jasper must've done before him.

This door opened into a room about the same size as the first one, but very different in setup. The steel walls were rough and unpainted; the wooden floorboards were scratched and worn. It was a cargo area. Coils of ropes hung from hooks on one wall, and a few pieces of packing crate were strewn around. But what caught Sam's attention were the large white mounds dotting the room. It looked like someone had tried to make volcanoes out of mashed potatoes. Sam was so distracted by the scene, he walked right into the small gas tank sitting near the door. It was an acetylene torch unit for cutting steel, and it was brand new. That explained the hole in the smokestack, Sam thought as he turned his attention back to the small white hills. He remembered Jenny telling him the *Panehesy* had been carrying medical supplies. Could the white mounds be soggy bedding and bandages? The room was damp, and when Sam aimed his flashlight upward, he found the source. A big, rusty wound had formed in the ceiling. Seventy-three years' worth of winter rainfall had seeped down into the *Panehesy* and worked its way through the roof above the cargo area. Over the years the bandages had soaked it up and turned to white sludge.

Thanks to the damp there was no magic dust in the cargo room, so no prints to follow, but as Sam neared the center of the space, he got a terrifying feeling he knew what had happened. Not all the moisture had been absorbed by the bandages. Hidden behind one of the soggy hills was a gaping hole—the kind that had to have been made by something or some*one* falling through the rotten floorboards. As if to confirm that, the boards below Sam's feet began to creak, sending him shuffling for safer ground near the wall.

A search for another way down turned up nothing, and Sam soon found himself back at the hole. The coiled ropes were still in good condition, and Sam tied one to a metal ring welded to the wall. With no way of knowing if more of the floor would collapse, Sam opted to go on his stomach, feetfirst. He slithered backward until enough of his body was in the hole for gravity to take hold. The planks under him groaned, and when a sharp splintering sound echoed around him, Sam could do nothing but shut his eyes and prepare for the worst. The noises died away. Sam hung there, feeling his hands burning from holding the rope so tightly. Slowly, he inched his way down until he felt his boots make contact with the floor. The room below had a steel floor, or, at least, there was steel underneath the layer of debris that had come down with the roof. Sam turned on his flashlight and looked down at the crude circle of rotten floorboards around him, but then the beam of his light hit something else.

He stumbled out of the wood pile and ran to the lifeless, blood-splattered body. Sam dropped to his knees, and the dull *thud* as he hit the steel floor echoed through the ship. It was as if the *Panehesy* were acknowledging Sam's loss. He hadn't dared contemplate this moment. He hadn't been brave enough.

As he reached out and laid a hand on the cold, lifeless body, he felt his world collapsing around him. Jasper hadn't died straightaway. His small daypack was rolled up like a pillow behind his head. In his last moment he had tried to get comfortable. He had also written something. The piece of paper was resting in his hand on top of his blood-soaked shirt.

THIS IS THE LAST WILL AND TESTAMENT
JASPER FORCE

I DIED HERE ~~TUESDAY JULY 28~~
~~WED JULY 29~~
THU JULY 30

PLEASE CONTACT FRANCIS VERULAM OF THE
VERULAM CORPORATION AND TELL HIM MY
DYING WISH WAS THAT MY NEPHEW SAM
FORCE BE TOLD THE WHOLE TRUTH.

As Sam stared at his uncle's final words, a cough startled him. Slowly, he lowered the note and saw two big blue eyes staring right at him.

"Not you again," said Jasper, almost in disgust. And then his eyes shut, as if he was going back to sleep or being dead, leaving Sam, kneeling next to him, stunned.

"Uncle Jasper, it's me," he said nervously, wondering if it was his mind playing some sick trick on him.

Jasper's eyes stayed shut, but he replied angrily, "I know who you are, and I'm not interested."

"Not interested? In what?"

"Having a conversation with my imagination. Now GO AWAY!"

"Jasper, it's me," said Sam, placing his hand gently on his uncle's arm.

The act had an instant effect. Jasper's eyes opened and locked on to Sam. But differently this time. More intensely. Then the stern lines on his face melted away, and when he spoke, it was almost a whisper. "Sam? Is that really you?"

"Of course it is. Who did you think it was?"

"The other Sam. I mean the you . . . in my imagination. You've been to visit me a few times since my accident."

"What happened to you? I thought you were dead. . . . I mean, all the blood . . . I checked your pulse on your neck, like they do on TV, but I couldn't feel anything. And you were cold. I was sure you were dead." The words tumbled out of Sam's mouth in one nervous download.

Jasper smiled. "Well, despite your diagnosis, I'm happy to say I'm alive," he said, then pointed to his legs. "But not without injury, I'm afraid. Broken in three places, from what I have been able to work out."

"But what about all the blood?" asked Sam, aiming the flashlight at his uncle's T-shirt, which was caked in the stuff.

Jasper winced. "Ah yes, well, that's a bit embarrassing actually. I landed nose first when I fell through the ceiling. I managed to clean my face up a bit, but it's amazing how much claret comes out of the old hooter, isn't it?"

Sam shook his head. He couldn't believe he was having this conversation. Seconds ago he had lost his uncle, been alone in the world. Now everything had changed. "I need to get you out of here."

"Yes, yes, all in good time, my boy," said Jasper as if Sam had walked into a coffee shop to fetch him. "But first tell me how on earth you managed to find me here in the *Panehesy*. In Egypt, for that matter. I sent you an e-mail telling you not to come."

"I know," said Sam, "but someone made sure I didn't get it."

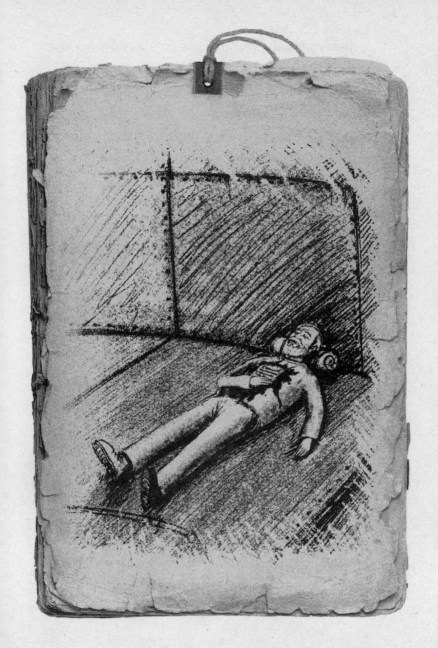

Jasper nodded. "I see. But, my boy, how did you ever manage to track me down to this godforsaken spot?"

Sam smiled. "I guess spending all that time watching you work taught me a thing or two, eh?"

"Quite. I encrypted the results of my research in case they fell into the wrong hands. I thought I'd done quite a good job."

"Hey, I'm not saying it was easy."

"Well, it was lucky for me, because I don't mind admitting that I had resigned myself to the fact that I was going to end my days in this rusty tomb."

"I know." Sam held up the bloodstained note. "I read your will. What was with the date changes?"

"I found myself slipping in and out of consciousness, and each time I thought maybe that was going to be the last. Besides"—Jasper chuckled and patted his old digital wristwatch—"you know us Egyptologists are sticklers for accurate dates."

"Dates. Sure," said Sam as he ran his flashlight around the empty cargo hold. "Nineteen forty-two. That was a date I worked out all by myself." It was no time to brag, but Sam couldn't help himself.

"Yes, you did." Jasper reached out and patted Sam on the head affectionately. "Tell me, what else do you know about this little adventure we both find ourselves on?"

"I know it's about Akhenaten, alchemy, and possibly the pyramids."

Jasper's eyes lit up. "Good, Sam. Very good. We'll start with Akhenaten. His ideas were controversial, and his reign came to an end when he was forced to abdicate. He fled into the Sinai Desert with a few of his followers, but I don't think he left empty-handed."

"Okay . . ." Sam waited for his uncle to elaborate.

"There's another famous character who fled from Egypt into the Sinai with his followers. Do you know who?"

Sam shook his head.

"Moses."

"Moses . . . as in the Ten Commandments Moses?"

"Exactly."

Sam was getting more confused by the second, and he wasn't in the mood for one of Jasper's "make history fun" lessons. "Look, we can talk about this later. Why don't we get you out of here." He pulled the GPS out of his backpack, but that just seemed to annoy Jasper.

"My boy, I have been stuck down here for three days. I can wait a little longer. Don't you want to know what I've discovered? Besides," he said, pointing to the GPS, "you'll have to go back up to the surface to get a signal."

Sam looked at the screen and saw his uncle was

right. "Okay, fine. Tell me about Moses. Where does he fit into all this?"

"Moses was banished from Egypt and fled into the Sinai with his followers. But he had one very special object with him. Remember what it was?"

"The Ark," said Sam. "The Ark of the . . ."

"Covenant. That's right."

"So, let me get this straight. You think Akhenaten was Moses and that he took off with the Ark?"

Uncle Jasper broke out one of his whiskery grins. "Quite possibly." He reached behind and pulled a piece of paper out of his daypack. His eyes sparkled as he handed it to Sam. "Read this."

The Ark of the Covenant

The word "Ark" comes from the Hebrew word
Aron, which means a chest or box, and was
described in the Bible as a sacred container for the
Ten Commandments as well as Aaron's rod and
a golden jar containing manna.

*The Ark was described as being made of shittah
tree wood (acacia)—known to the Egyptians as the
Tree of Life—and covered with the purest gold.*

"But you said this was about alchemy. So . . . does
the Ark hold the secret of how to turn lead into gold?"

"The secret to alchemy, yes—or at least, that's what
many believe. But this is far bigger than gold."

"What could be bigger than gold?"

"Eternal life."

Sam wondered if his uncle had suffered a serious
blow to the head. "You're telling me the Ark is some
kind of fountain of youth?"

Jasper must have picked up the sarcasm in Sam's
voice, because he shrugged. "Probably not. It seems too
unbelievable, yes? But there are enough people who
believe it to be true that they've spent their lives searching for it."

"But why you? You risked *your* life to find it. What
do you want with it?"

"Fountain of youth or not, the Ark is a priceless
treasure, Sam. It may contain clues that could finally
tell us why the pyramids were built. For centuries, man
has studied the pyramids, hoping to discover the reason
for their existence. I believe the Ark will tell us."

Jasper reached back into his bag again and pulled

out his flashlight. It was smaller than Sam's, but packed a much better punch. He aimed it toward the front of the ship, and caught in its beam was the only object in the cavernous space. An old wooden crate, secured to the deck with ropes, measuring what Sam guessed to be slightly bigger than 2.5 cubits by 1.5 cubits by 1.5 cubits.

Jasper opened his mouth to speak, but before he could, his face contorted in agony. Despite his uncle's chatty demeanor it was obvious to Sam that he had been trying to hide just how much pain he was in.

"Okay, that's it," said Sam. "I'm getting help."

Jasper didn't argue this time. He lay back and took a series of short, deep breaths. "Okay . . . fine . . . I'll . . . wait here."

You have to admire the guy, thought Sam. Near death and still trying to crack jokes. "I'll be back soon, Jasper. I'll make the call, and help will be here quick."

Sam wasn't sure if his uncle heard him. His eyes had shut and his breathing had steadied. He'd passed out again.

THE DECISION TO TAKE JASPER'S FLASH- light paid off when Sam spotted a ladder on the back wall. It made the climb back through the hole a little easier and cleaner. On the upper level Sam ran down the corridor, ripped open the door to the dining room, and froze. A massive ball of light was hovering in the middle of the room. Sam threw up his arms to shield his eyes, but the glare had already blinded him temporarily.

"Who is it?" he called out. "Who's there?"

The glowing orb dropped away as the high-powered flashlight was pointed at the floor. Sam couldn't see, but there was no mistaking the voice that echoed across the dining room.

"Sam, my friend. Hello there."

It was Cairo's craziest taxi driver.

21

THE END OF
THE LIE

SAM WAS TOO STUNNED TO SPEAK. THE
last time they'd seen each other, Hadi had been sliding
a sewer lid closed. Now, here he was on the *Panehesy*
with the same toothy grin.

"Surprised to see me, eh?"

Sam nodded slowly at the understatement.
"What . . . ?" Sam tried to string some words together,
but they wouldn't come out. Hadi wasn't moving. He
just stood there smiling. But while it was the same
familiar grin, something wasn't quite right. The fact he
was there at all, on a ship buried in the desert, wasn't

right, but there was something else. And then it clicked.

Hadi was waiting for someone.

Sam glanced past the Egyptian to the black hole that had been cut in the smokestack, but the darkness was fading away as someone with a flashlight came down the rope. A body dropped into the space, and a third person entered the dining room. It was another familiar face, but this one wasn't smiling.

"We missed each other at the Al Minya Museum," the Short-Haired Man said. "It's nice to finally catch up with you."

Sam's gaze flicked between the two faces, trying to make sense of what he was seeing, but it was Hadi's uncomfortable look that helped him put it together.

"You were working for him all along," Sam said, bringing his flashlight back to the underage taxi driver.

Hadi seemed to squirm in the light. "It was a job, my friend," he offered apologetically. "Just a job."

The Short-Haired Man laughed as he stepped up beside Hadi and thrust his arm roughly around the boy's shoulders. "And a very good job you did too."

Hadi didn't seem comfortable with the praise or the rough embrace, but the Short-Haired Man was enjoying Sam's obvious shock.

"A complete stranger so eager to help you? Please," he scoffed. "You didn't stop to think it was all . . . what is the saying? Too good to be true?" He let out another throaty laugh, and Hadi tried to pry himself free, but the Short-Haired Man clutched him firmly.

"When I lost you in the market, Sam, I sent young Hadi in to sniff you out. But I heard it was you who found him." He laughed and waited for Sam to say something, but didn't seem put off by the stony silence. "The driver heading to Al Minya, the one Hadi just happened to know—you didn't stop to think perhaps you were a little too lucky?" The Short-Haired Man shook his head. "No, you didn't, did you? You know, it was all a bit of a rush to pull that together. Especially Hadi's special present."

"What present?"

The Short-Haired Man was happy to have gotten a response. "What present? Why, your necklace, of course. Do you still have it on? Of course you do." He grinned and pulled a small black box out of his pocket and held it out for Sam to see. "We wouldn't have been able to track you here if you didn't."

Hadi squirmed as the man continued.

"I'll admit," he said, inspecting the unit in his hand, "I should have had more faith in this technology. Coming for you at the museum was a mistake. I almost scared you off, yes?"

It was a rhetorical question, but Sam couldn't help

himself. "You didn't scare me off." He spat the words out. "I managed to get rid of you a couple of times. Same with your boss with the beard."

"He's not my boss." The Short-Haired Man growled and took another step toward Sam. "We work for the same people, but I work alone." The smirk had left his face. He was rattled, and his anger was showing, "The fact remains," he continued, "that I found you in the end. Enough of this. Time is wasting. Where's your uncle and where's the artifact?"

"I don't—"

Sam didn't see it coming. The lightning-fast slap across his face sounded like a snapping stick in the confines of the dining room. His vision clouded; his eyes watered.

"Time is wasting. Let's go," the Short-Haired Man said, shoving Sam toward the corridor.

JASPER WAS STILL UNCONSCIOUS, BUT for all the Short-Haired Man knew he could have been dead.

"This one was harder to track than you, Sam. After we arranged the theft from the EEF bank account, we hoped the police might do the job for us. When we intercepted his e-mail to you, we saw a way you could help." He turned to Sam. "And you have been a great help," he sneered. "Now, where is the artifact?"

Sam swung his flashlight toward the wooden crate. The Short-Haired Man clapped his hands together and grinned like a child as he pushed past Sam and Hadi.

Sam watched the man walk up to the crate and pat it as if it were a large dog.

"I had arranged for a couple of men to remove this," he called over his shoulder, "but one had a nasty motorbike accident in town, and the other seems to have gone missing in the desert."

"What a shame," said Sam through gritted teeth.

The Short-Haired Man turned and leaned back on the crate. "It's of no consequence. I have achieved my goal, and I have two able-bodied helpers right here, don't I?"

"If I help you get it out, will you promise to get help for my uncle?"

The Short-Haired Man glanced at Jasper, then waved his helpers to the Ark. "Come," he ordered. "We'll discuss that when the job is done."

IT WAS SURPRISINGLY LIGHT FOR ITS size, and inside the crate could well be one of the world's great hidden treasures, but all Sam cared about was getting his uncle to safety. The Short-Haired Man, the guy with the beard, and whoever they worked for, were welcome to the crate itself.

The hardest part was getting the crate up through the hole in the ceiling. Hadi and Sam worked together at the bottom while the Short-Haired Man rigged a crane using some of the ropes. They worked in near silence; at one point Hadi offered a hushed apology and something about needing the money, but Sam ignored him.

In the dining room the problem of how the crate was supposed to fit through a person-sized hole in the smokestack was solved when the Short-Haired Man produced what looked like a gun from his pocket. When he pulled the trigger, a bright blue flame appeared at the end of the barrel. It made short work of the steel, slicing through it as if it were balsa wood. Then, once the ropes were attached again, Hadi climbed out to haul the crate up.

SAM STOOD NEAR THE SMOKESTACK, listening to the echoey thumps and scraping sounds subside as Hadi hauled the *Panehesy*'s treasure to the surface.

"Now we need to get my uncle," he said.

The Short-Haired Man had taken a seat at one of the tables, seventy-three years too late for a meal, but now he shot to his feet, kicking the chair with the back of his boot so it skidded across the floor and smashed into the wall. "What I need to do . . . is contact my employers and tell them I have secured their cargo."

"But you said you'd help my uncle," insisted Sam. "If we don't get him out of here, he'll die!"

"You really have no idea what you're involved in, do you?"

"I know that crate contains the Ark of the Covenant," Sam said defiantly.

"Very good," sneered the Short-Haired Man. "Then you must also realize that you and your uncle know too much. My employers were very clear, Sam. Collect the artifact, then tie up the loose ends. And you," he said, jabbing a finger at Sam, "are a loose end."

More banging and scraping sounds filled the dining room as Hadi climbed back in through the new and improved hole.

"What do you think you're doing?" the Short-Haired Man asked.

"I came to help with Sam's uncle."

"Search him," came the hissed reply.

Hadi shuffled over to Sam and patted him down awkwardly. He passed the GPS phone to the Short-Haired Man, who appeared to fumble and drop it.

"Oh dear," he muttered sarcastically before he lifted

one leg and brought the heel of his boot smashing down onto the phone, sending shards of plastic skidding across the floor. "Go back up and wait for me," he said to Hadi as he admired his work.

"But what about—"

Hadi was cut off when the Short-Haired Man hit him in the face.

"Get up top now, or die here with your friend."

Hadi eyed his attacker through blood-covered fingers as he tried to stem the gush coming from the pulpy mess that had been his nose. Then, without looking at Sam, he climbed back into the smokestack.

The Short-Haired Man followed, stopping briefly to speak one last time before he grabbed the rope. "You should leave the room too, Sam," he said without a trace of remorse. "It's going to get a bit messy in here."

A few minutes later Sam heard the metallic *thumps* of the charges being placed. When it came, the muffled *boom* wasn't as loud as he had been expecting, but the explosion blasted the sand in the smokestack out of the hole and into the dining room, like steam out of a geyser. It came thick and fast and with so much power Sam was knocked off his feet as a wall of sand and smoke spewed over him and rolled down the corridor.

When the air had cleared enough for Sam to see,

the dining room had been transformed into an indoor desert. A thick layer of sand led to a sloping wall of the stuff where the smokestack had been moments ago. The only way out of the *Panehesy* had been destroyed. Just like Sam's hope of saving his uncle.

22

SEEDS OF DESTRUCTION

JASPER WAS CONSCIOUS WHEN SAM GOT back to him, but only just. His breathing was shallow. His face was bathed in sweat.

"Sam, you're okay. Thank goodness," Jasper said, gasping for air. "I heard an explosion."

"We're trapped," Sam said. There didn't seem to be any point in trying to soften the story. "I was followed by someone. Someone I thought was trying to help me." He ripped off the scarab necklace and tossed it into the dark recesses of the cargo hold. "They blew up the smokestack."

"And the Ark?" asked Jasper.

"Gone."

Jasper lowered his head and took a series of slow, labored breaths. "I'm sorry for dragging you into this, my boy," he wheezed. "Truly sorry."

Sam leaned back against the steel hull. "How did this happen, Jasper? I mean . . . if you knew it was getting dangerous, why did you go on?"

There was silence as Jasper built up the energy to reply. "There's a man called Francis Verulam. A couple of weeks ago he told me he had important information about a theory regarding the truth behind the pyramids. He believes they have a sacred heart—a battery, if you will—that belongs inside them."

"And he thinks the Ark is that sacred heart?"

Jasper took another deep breath. "Correct."

"I've met his daughter," said Sam. "Mary Verulam. She was sitting next to me on the flight. Turned out her father sent her to keep an eye me."

Jasper reached out for Sam's hand. It was clammy and trembling. "My boy, we're involved in something far bigger than I ever imagined. I really am sorry for dragging you into it."

"You keep saying that, but why did you?" Sam was getting angry. "You found the missing Ark, but was it worth all this?" He thumped the steel floor. "You could have just said no to Francis Verulam." Sam felt bad losing his cool, but he figured he'd earned the right. After all, they were both going to die.

"I'll admit it, Sam. Mr. Verulam's theory was interesting," said Jasper, "but that's not why I took the assignment."

"Why? Because he pays my school fees?"

"In a way. I understood that the Verulam Corporation paid your school fees because Francis Verulam had been a friend of your parents, but there was more to their relationship, and it has something to do with what really happened to them."

Sam shined his flashlight into Jasper's eyes to see if he was delirious. "What are you talking about? My parents were murdered while they were on vacation in Jamaica. You told me that."

"I know, I know, Sam. That's what I was told—and believed—until I spoke to Mr. Verulam."

Jasper gritted his teeth and threw his head back as his body was racked by another wave of pain. The first thought through Sam's mind was that his uncle might pass out or even die before he explained himself, and he was immediately disgusted by that reaction. "Jasper, what can I do for you?" he said urgently. "Tell me, please."

Jasper grabbed his arm, surprising Sam with the

strength he'd suddenly found. "Nothing, my boy." His face relaxed as the pain passed. "Listen to me. I need to tell you the whole truth now, while I still can."

Sam thought back to the bloody note he had found when he arrived.

"Your parents weren't on vacation in Jamaica. They weren't even in Jamaica. I only found that out when Mr. Verulam contacted me. You remember I told you that your father left the EEF?"

Sam nodded.

"He didn't leave, Sam. He was fired. Your parents told me they were taking a break in Jamaica to reassess their priorities, but I know now they lied, probably to protect me from any fallout."

"Why was he fired?"

"Both your parents believed there was a link between the ancient pyramids around the world."

"Around the world? You mean Egypt?"

"No, Sam. Beyond Egypt, giant pyramids have been found in South America, Europe, even China. But the EEF doesn't take kindly to that line of thinking. Your father was given repeated warnings to drop his investigations, and when he wouldn't, he was fired. But it seems Mr. Verulam offered to fund his research. *He* was behind your parents' trip to South America."

"South America?!"

"Yes. They were in South America when they disappeared."

"You said this hunt for the *Panehesy* has something to do with them. What?"

Jasper sighed again. "I'm not sure exactly, Sam. Mr. Verulam said the *Panehesy* was linked to your parents' disappearance. He implied that finding it might give us some answers."

Sam tried to process what he was hearing about his parents, and about pyramids around the world. Just when he thought he was starting to understand what was going on, it got more complicated. "You know, Mary told me her grandfather Jason Verulam had some crazy theories about the pyramids."

"Maybe not so crazy after all."

Sam nodded. "Mary also said that her grandfather died this year, and soon after that her father found out about the *Panehesy*. Maybe Jason Verulam knew it was here?"

"Interesting," Jasper said. "But I don't think Jason Verulam just *knew* about the *Panehesy*. Look what I found on the crate when I arrived."

From the seeds of our destruction grows hope of our escape

JV June 21 1942

"That's the logo on the letter Francis Verulam sent you," said Sam.

"Indeed. And I think it is safe to assume *JV* is Jason Verulam. But look at the date."

"June twenty-first."

"I take it the lovely Ms. Cole told you about the great storm."

"Who?"

"The charming curator of the Al Minya Museum."

"Oh . . . her. Sure." Sam was put off by the strange look on his uncle's face. "She said it started June eighteenth and lasted five days."

"Wiping away all trace of the *Panehesy*," Jasper chipped in. "So, if Jason Verulam was here on June twenty-first . . ."

"He must have found a way out," said Sam.

"Exactly, my boy."

"Could he have gotten out the way you came in?"

Jasper shook his head. "Not a chance. I had to cut through the metal rain plate at the top of the smokestack to get in."

Sam looked at the note again. "*From the seeds of our destruction* . . . Hang on. In the port log it said that the *Panehesy* was damaged by an explosion in the boiler room that blew a hole in the hull."

Jasper managed a weak smile. "You were paying

attention, weren't you? But I'm not surprised. Ms. Cole was a charm, wasn't she?"

Sam shook his head in disbelief. "Uncle Jasper, think you can keep your mind on the job? We're in a bit of trouble here."

"Certainly, my boy." Jasper laughed weakly. "But when we get out, remind me to send that lovely lady some flowers." He threw in a wink, which seemed almost comical coming from a man in such bad shape. "Flowers, Sam, are the true way to a woman's heart."

The talk of Jenny seemed to have cheered Jasper up, and Sam was glad about that, but he could tell his uncle was still trying to hide how much pain he was in.

"*From the seeds of our destruction grows our hope of escape,*" repeated Jasper as he delved back into his bag. "I found this when I was in Alexandria."

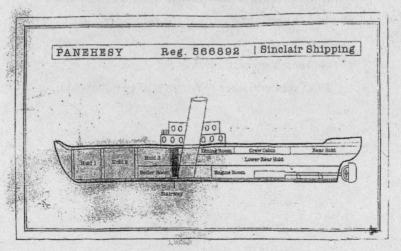

PANEHESY   Reg. 566892 | Sinclair Shipping

Sam studied the cross section of the *Panehesy*. "You think the hole in the boiler room was how he got out?"

Jasper nodded.

"You had already worked this all out, hadn't you?" said Sam.

"Well, I have had a bit of time on my hands."

"Then, I need to get down there and check it out."

"Ah."

"That doesn't sound like a very confident 'ah,'" Sam said.

"No, it's not, I'm afraid. Seventy-three years ago there was a stairwell that went from the top to the bottom of the ship. You can see it on the map. But it's full of sand now. I know, because I checked when I was looking for a way down here. The smokestack would have been the same if the rain plate hadn't been in place."

"So there's no way down?"

"No," replied Jasper. "You're going to have to make one."

23

DEAD MAN'S PASSAGE

SAM RETURNED TO THE UPPER DECK AND used one of the coils of rope on the wall to lower the acetylene torch down through the hole in the floor. Compared to the high-tech device the Short-Haired Man had used, Jasper's unit was slow. Not so much a hot knife through butter as a blunt knife through wood. Clouds of yellow sparks lit up the space like fireworks set off in a closet, and as Sam worked behind the plastic mask he'd found next to the unit, he discovered that there was more to cutting plate steel than meets the eye. The finished hole made the one his uncle had cut look like a masterpiece.

The ropes that had held the Ark's crate in place were still secured to the floor, so Sam tossed one into the nasty-looking hole and prepared for the descent.

"See ya soon," he called to his uncle. There was no response. After his spirited conversation about Jenny from the museum, Jasper had gone downhill. He was about to pass out again, but Sam thought that might be for the best. Lying there, bathed in the yellow glow of the flashlight, his uncle looked like a corpse. Their discussion, combined with Jasper's efforts to disguise the pain he was in, had taken a heavy toll. But even then, he had still tried to turn the situation into a lesson. He'd already worked out that Jason Verulam had escaped from the *Panehesy*; he could have simply blurted it out. Instead, he'd helped Sam reach that conclusion himself.

That need to turn everything into a school lesson had always infuriated Sam, but standing there, by the edge of the crudely cut hole, he saw his uncle in a new light. It wasn't that Jasper simply liked playing the role of teacher, Sam realized. Everything he did was born from a desire to help Sam learn to think for himself. To help him make his way in the world. That independent spirit that Sam prided himself on? His uncle had helped to nurture that. Sam had been joking when he told Jasper he had picked up a few things from him over the years, but he knew that statement was true. This adventure, the fact he had made it this far, was because of the training and teaching his uncle had given him. This was the gift his uncle had to offer, and he had done so willingly, for years, despite Sam's lack of gratitude.

Sam suddenly felt closer to his uncle than ever before. He wanted to run over and tell him how much he loved him, thank him for the years of attention and affection, but he didn't. The thank-yous and apologies could wait until he and Jasper were free.

Sam grabbed the thick hemp rope and slid down into the deepest depths of the *Panehesy*.

HE LANDED IN ANOTHER DARK HOLE, BUT knew it was different even before he switched on the flashlight. The stench of diesel fuel made him long for the musty, stale air of the cargo deck. The beam from his flashlight stabbed across the floor, exposing a room packed with the rusting carcasses of what had once been engines. Compared to the open expanse of the deck above, the space was cramped. Pipes lined each side of the room and disappeared through the wall. Sand spilling out through the open door hinted that the desert had already claimed the boiler room for itself, but when Sam looked closer, he saw that it hadn't. He stepped into the room and saw that the sand was the work of men—and one of them was still there.

The skeleton was wearing faded rags that had once been shorts, but the bones looked like they had been shrink-wrapped in brown plastic. If it had been hanging in a costume shop, Sam would have complained that the thing looked way too fake.

But this was real. Seventy-three years in a temperature-controlled environment had mummified the body, *Panehesy* style. The flesh had melted away, leaving the skin to form a crispy brown layer over the bones. Sam stared at the body perched on its throne of sand, and it gazed back through the sunken hollows that had once contained eyes. There was a strange-looking pistol lying next to it. It was made of dull brass and had a short, wide barrel.

There was so much sand in the room, it took a few seconds to locate the source. The canvas curtain was almost the same color as the wall. Sam pulled it back to reveal the manhole-sized gouge that had been made by the explosion. Another tattered piece of canvas had been laid across the bottom edge of the hole. Lying there, hanging out of the tunnel, it looked like a leathery tongue of some prehistoric monster. The *Panehesy* had failed to claim Sam; now the desert was inviting him in to try his luck there.

As Sam looked around the boiler room that had become a burial chamber, his flashlight lit up a dusty red notebook sitting on the iron beam above the door. Sam took the book down and opened it. The faded handwriting was barley legible on the brittle yellow pages, but as Sam began reading, he realized he was holding the dairy of the man whose footsteps he was about to follow.

June 17

The explosion was no accident.

I suspected this from the start, and a closer inspection, when we docked in Al Minya, confirmed my fears. A reminder, if needed, of the importance of this mission and the forces that plot to stop us.

The Port Master has ordered us upstream to a mooring barge. One of the crew was behind the bomb. I have no way of knowing who, so I have off-loaded them all. Only Thomas has remained with me, but this means it will take more than one night to make the repairs we need to get us back to Alexandria safely.

June 18

A massive storm has hit us. I've never seen anything like it. A thick brown soup has enveloped the Panehesy, obscuring all vision. She is an old girl, and the bridge and officers' quarters are of flimsy wooden construction. In this howling gale, they creak and groan under the high winds that batter us without reprieve. In an effort to find a little more peace, Thomas and I have retreated belowdecks. The only consolation of this horrific weather is that our enemies are as blinded as we are, and this works to ensure the success of my great deception.

June 19

It seems our move was timely. During the night I feared the Panehesy was breaking up, as the sound of splintering timber and smashing glass joined the hellish din made by the winds that raged around us. We survived, but with the day came the discovery that the entire structure above deck has been washed away by a sea of

SAND. THIS WE CAN live WITHOUT, BUT ANOTHER
CASUALTY OF THE NIGHT WAS THE WATER TANK
THAT STOOD AT THE BACK OF THE SHIP. ALL WE
HAVE LEFT TO DRINK IS THE WATER THAT REMAINED
IN THE PIPES. IT FILLED TWO SMALL BOTTLES. UNTIL
NOW THIS STORM HAS MERELY BEEN INCONVENIENT.
IF IT GOES ON MUCH LONGER, IT COULD BECOME A
FAR GREATER THREAT.

JUNE 20

THE SUN DIDN'T RISE TODAY. I THOUGHT PERHAPS
MY WATCH WAS WRONG, AND THEN WE DISCOVERED,
TO OUR HORROR, THAT THE BLACKNESS OUTSIDE THE
POTHOLES IS NOT NIGHT, BUT SAND.

THE LAST OF OUR FOOD HAS GONE, BUT IT IS OUR
LACK OF WATER THAT HANGS OVER US LIKE THE
SWORD OF DAMOCLES. THE STORM STILL RAGES,
ALBEIT A LITTLE QUIETER NOW. BUT I FEAR THIS IS
NOT A SIGN THAT IT IS WEAKENING, RATHER THE
DEADENING OF THE NOISE AS THE SAND BUILDS UP
AROUND US.

WE ARE BEING BURIED ALIVE.

June 21

A DEATHLY SILENCE GREETED US WHEN WE AWOKE
THIS MORNING. IS THIS A SIGN THE STORM HAS
FINISHED? WE HAVE NO WAY OF KNOWING. THE DOOR
TO THE STAIRS THAT LEADS TO THE DECK IS BLOCKED.
THE DESERT HAS SEALED US IN AS SURELY AS THE
LOCK ON A CAGE.

I SEE THE PANIC IN THOMAS'S EYES EVEN THOUGH HE
WORKS TO HIDE IT. I HOPE I'M DOING A BETTER JOB
THAN HIM.

I CAN FEEL MY SANITY BEING SUCKED UP LIKE THE AIR
IN HERE. HOW MUCH IS THERE? WILL THAT BE OUR
UNDOING? NO MATTER! TO WRITE OF THESE THINGS
IS AS POISONOUS AS THINKING THEM. OUR EFFORTS
MUST GO INTO OUR ESCAPE.

FROM THE SEEDS OF OUR DESTRUCTION!

I HAD PLACED SOME BOARDS OVER THE HOLE MADE BY
THE EXPLOSION, AND NOW IT SEEMS IT IS THE ONLY
WAY OUT OF THIS IRON TOMB. WE CAN DIG THROUGH
SAND AND WE HAVE WOOD FOR SHORING THE TUNNEL,

THANKS TO THE CRATE IN THE REAR CARGO DECK.
WHAT WE DON'T HAVE IS AN ABUNDANCE OF TIME.
SO WE WILL DIG AND DIG AND FREE OURSELVES FROM
HERE. OR DIE TRYING.

JUNE 22

WE ARE AT LEAST 40 FEET UNDERGROUND, BUT
IT HAS PROVED IMPOSSIBLE TO DIG STRAIGHT UP. OUR
ONLY HOPE IS A TUNNEL THAT SLOPES UP GRADUALLY TO
THE SURFACE. WE WORK ONE-HOUR ON, ONE-HOUR
OFF. IT MEANS OUR PROGRESS IS PAINFULLY SLOW,
BUT IN OUR WEAKENED STATE THIS IS ALL WE CAN
HANDLE. I MANAGED TO DRAIN THE LAST DREGS OF
WATER FROM THE BOILER. A RUSTY ORANGE SOUP, IT
SMELLS PUTRID AND IS BITTER TO THE TONGUE, BUT IF
THIS SUSTAINS US EVEN ONE DAY LONGER, THEN WE
ACCEPT IT GRATEFULLY.

OUR TUNNEL IS A CRUDE AFFAIR, JUST WIDE ENOUGH
FOR ONE. WE TAKE TURNS TO DIG WHILE THE OTHER
CARRIES THE SAND BACK INTO THE ENGINE ROOM IN
THE CANVAS FIRE BUCKET.

I TRIED TO SPECULATE WITH THOMAS TODAY AS TO
WHICH MEMBER OF THE CREW WAS THE TRAITOR. HE

SEEMED UNINTERESTED IN THE CONVERSATION. HE AND I WERE THE ONLY TWO LEFT ON BOARD WHO KNEW OF THE SECRET BURIED IN THE SANDS FOR OVER TWO AND A HALF THOUSAND YEARS. NOW WE FIGHT TO AVOID THE SAME FATE.

JUNE 23

WE ARE DYING. HOUR BY HOUR. NEITHER OF US SPEAKS OF IT: IN FACT, WE SPEAK VERY LITTLE NOW. THOMAS SITS IN SILENCE, WATCHING ME WRITE. HE ASKED WHY I SIT HERE SCRIBBLING OBSESSIVELY. A LINK TO NORMALCY? A CHANCE TO POUR FORTH THE WORDS THAT NO LONGER COME FROM MY SWOLLEN TONGUE? 'TIS NOT DEATH I FEAR. IT IS THE IDEA THAT MY KNOWLEDGE WILL BE BURIED HERE WITH ME. IF THIS IRON TOMB IS TO BECOME MY ETERNAL RESTING PLACE, THEN LET ME PUT HERE IN WRITING THAT WHICH HAS BEEN PASSED FROM MOUTH TO EAR FOR CENTURIES.

THAT THE KNIGHTS TEMPLAR DISCOVERED THE ARK OF THE COVENANT IN THE RUINS OF SOLOMON'S TEMPLE HAS BEEN THE SUBJECT OF SPECULATION BY MANY, AND IT IS TRUE. BUT THIS TREASURE WAS ONE OF TWO THEY FOUND.

The other was knowledge.

Knowledge that came from a story carved into the Ark. A story that told of heretic king Akhenaten, who stole the original Ark from its home in the heart of the Great Pyramid at Giza, and took it to his new city Amarna.

A secret few worked to overthrow him and reclaim this treasure and the powers it possessed.

Akhenaten, who the world came to know as Moses, fled to the desert with his followers, and it was here, history tells us, that the Ark was built. This was made possible only because his craftsmen had studied the original. And what happened to that? This was Akhenaten's great deception. It was hidden in the very city he fled from—Amarna.

This is the secret the Templars discovered. This knowledge, a sacred flame, kept alive in the shadows for hundreds of years. Protected from the descendants of Akhenaten's enemies, who

HAVE ALWAYS SOUGHT TO RECLAIM THE Ark FOR THEIR OWN MEANS.

IN Amarna, THE Ark WOULD LIE STILL IF IT WERE NOT FOR THE TIDES OF WAR SWEEPING THE PLANET AND FEARS OF THE GUARDIANS OF THE FLAME THAT Akhenaten's DECEPTION WAS ABOUT TO BE DISCOVERED.

I WAS ENTRUSTED TO REMOVE THIS SACRED OBJECT FROM ITS HIDING PLACE AND NOW, HAVING READ THE ENGRAVINGS ON THE ORIGINAL Ark, I HAVE THE NEXT PIECE OF THIS GREAT STORY. IT MUST NOT BE LOST, SO IF MY JOURNEY IN THIS MORTAL BODY ENDS HERE I MUST COMMIT MY KNOWLEDGE TO PAPER, LEST IT BE LOST FOREV————

Thomas WAS THE TRAITOR, AND NOW HE IS DEAD!

He BEGAN PACING THE ROOM NERVOUSLY AS I WROTE. It STRUCK ME AS ODD BECAUSE WE HAVE LITTLE STRENGTH TO WASTE.

IN HIS HANDS WAS THE FLARE GUN THAT WE FOUND ON THE BRIDGE. He FINGERED IT NERVOUSLY. I UNDERSTAND

NOW THAT HE WAS BUILDING HIMSELF UP TO COMMIT MURDER.

HE PLANNED MY DEATH FROM THE START. THAT I LIVED THIS LONG WAS ONLY BECAUSE HE KNEW HE NEEDED HELP TO BUILD THE TUNNEL.

BUT NOW WE ARE CLOSE TO COMPLETION. OR PERHAPS THOMAS WAS WORRIED HE MIGHT NOT HAVE THE STRENGTH TO DO AWAY WITH ME IF HE WAITED.

THIS, I SUSPECT, IS THE DILEMMA HE WRESTLED WITH AND NOW, AS HIS LIFELESS EYES STARE AT ME FROM THE OTHER SIDE OF THE ROOM, IT IS THE PROBLEM HIS BRAIN CAN TOY WITH FOR ETERNITY.

HE CAME AT ME AS I SAT, HEAD DOWN OVER THIS JOURNAL. BUT FOR THIS FLICKER OF SHADOWS AS HE STEPPED IN FRONT OF THE LANTERN, I MIGHT NEVER HAVE LOOKED UP.

THAT CURIOSITY SURELY SAVED MY LIFE.

OUR STRUGGLE MIGHT HAVE SEEMED COMICAL TO A BYSTANDER IN THE STEEL-WALLED CELL. TWO MEN,

SO WEAK, SO NEAR COMPLETE EXHAUSTION, THAT WE SEEMED TO FIGHT IN SLOW MOTION.

HIS BLOW GLANCED OFF MY HEAD, AND HE STUMBLED PAST ME AS I STRUGGLED TO MY FEET. A DEEP GASH HAD OPENED ABOVE MY BROW; MY BLOOD RAN FREELY. IT STRUCK ME AS ODD THAT IT SHOULD POUR WITH SUCH VIGOUR FROM A BODY SO CLOSE TO DEATH, BUT THE SALTY LIQUID THAT RAN DOWN MY FACE AND ACROSS MY LIPS SURELY ALTERED THE COURSE OF THOMAS'S DEED.

THERE WAS NO CONSCIOUS THOUGHT ON MY PART, ONLY AN ANIMAL HUNGER FOR NUTRIENTS IN THE SCARLET GORE THAT OOZED FROM ME. I SUSPECT I MADE THE MOST HORRIFIC SIGHT FOR THOMAS AS I STOOD THERE PAWING AT MY WOUND AND LICKING THE BLOOD OFF MY HANDS. HE SEEMED TRANSFIXED OR PERHAPS JUST TOO EXHAUSTED TO MOVE. WHATEVER THE REASON, HIS FAILURE TO CAPITALIZE ON MY DISTRACTION COST HIM DEARLY.

SPURRED ON BY THE SUSTENANCE FROM MY WOUND I GRABBED ONE OF THE BROKEN PIECES OF PACKING CRATE, PUSHED THOMAS DOWN WITH NO GREATER EFFORT THAN IF HE HAD BEEN A SMALL CHILD. THEN, WITH MY CRUDE SWORD AT HIS THROAT, I DEMANDED AN EXPLANATION.

He confessed to the riches he had been promised for betraying our mission.

With this admission, he sealed his fate. I drove the wooden stake into the jugular vein and watched as his life force spilled out of him. As I sit here now, his blood still flows. A rich red pool, creeping out from his body across the floor toward the tunnel, and my salvation.

June 24

I hit rock today, but this may prove to be a blessing. Using the rock face for support I can build a shaft that goes straight up. This will surely save time.

The work is slow. I am performing the tasks of two now. I can only clear a few buckets of sand before I must stop and ferry it back into the ship. If I don't, I will find myself trapped, with no way forward or back. But my spirits have been lifted. I have more energy now and can work with renewed sense of purpose.

I HAVE PLANNED FOR MY ESCAPE BY CONSTRUCTING A COVER FOR THE TUNNEL. A GAPING HOLE WOULD ATTRACT UNWANTED ATTENTION. I MUST NOT LOSE SIGHT OF WHY I AM HERE.

ENOUGH WORDS FOR NOW. A FEW MOMENTS OF SLEEP, THEN BACK TO MY HELLISH WORK.

Sam felt guilty flicking though the pages of Jason Verulam's diary. The story was intriguing, but the image of his uncle lying on the deck above him forced him back to his feet.

Kneeling by the hole, Sam shined the flashlight into the old tunnel. The pieces of packing crate lining the walls and roof were rough and uneven. There were gaps between the wooden slats, and a couple of them had broken, leaving piles of sand blocking the narrow escape route. Sam needed something he could use to clear the way. The only object left in the room was the skeleton of Thomas. After a close inspection Sam settled on a thighbone as the ideal tool to help him through the tunnel.

He was wrong.

24

BACK FROM
THE DEAD

THE TUNNEL HAD COLLAPSED ON SAM.
The desert had tried to claim him as one of its own,
and he should have been dead, but he wasn't. A matter
of inches had saved his life.

As the wood that was holding the roof came down,
one piece had knocked him unconscious, but a few
more fell in such a way that they formed a small pro-
tective area around his mouth. It was a tiny space,
but enough to hold back the sand and save Sam from
suffocation.

He came to in complete blackness and tried to move
his arms. One was trapped at his side, the other, holding

the thighbone, had been stretched out in front of him when the collapse happened. He was like a swimmer frozen midstroke. He could move the arm in front, so he gently felt the area around him, forming a picture of his surroundings in his mind.

The first thing he found were the shattered remains of his flashlight, but the good news was that the cave-in had been limited to the area he was in. The area ahead felt clear.

Sam dug his fingers into the sand and tried to pull himself forward. His body slid a few inches before a sharp cracking sound filled the tiny chamber around him. Sam ducked his head and prepared for another avalanche of sand. When it didn't come, he sank his claw-shaped hand into the sand and pulled again.

Inch by inch Sam extracted himself from the tunnel's death hold, always listening for the crack that would signal his doom. But it never came. Instead, his other arm slipped free and he was able to pull himself out of the debris. But as he crawled forward, he became aware of a new threat: the floor of the tunnel was sloping up sharply. Sam was still on his stomach, but the roof was only a few inches above his head. A seventy-three-year-old ceiling that was probably so fragile the lightest touch could bring it down.

Sam had been so focused on getting free of the cave-in,

his mind hadn't given him time to stop to dwell on his situation—that he was trapped in the dark in a space no bigger than a coffin, God knows how far under the desert. But now, as he lay there sucking in the warm, fetid air, the panic demons came banging on his door with a vengeance, demanding to be let in, to be heard.

This will be the end. The thought came to him as clear as day. If he let panic take over, he would die there, and it all would have been for nothing.

Sam closed his eyes, knowing it was pointless, given there was absolutely no difference between having them open or shut, but as he lay there and breathed slowly, he felt better. The panic didn't dissolve to nothing, just faded to a dull throb far enough away to let Sam think.

The roof was intact. The extra sand wasn't the result of a cave-in. What did he know about the tunnel? Jason Verulam had finished it himself, swapping between digging and clearing. In his last entry he had started the shaft, but he had never finished the journal. Why not? Had he given up on clearing the sand? Simply pushed it behind him in his last frantic attempt to get free?

Sam rolled onto his side and began to carefully sweep the sand down past him. His movements were slow and gentle, the way he had seen his uncle uncovering remains in the desert. But the stakes were far higher here. One rough move and the roof would violently end its seventy-three-year run.

Once again it was Sam's hands that told him what was happening. The gap in front was getting bigger. Soon there was enough room for Sam to edge forward without touching the roof. He swept more sand back and slid forward inch by inch until his hand hit rock.

Sam raised his right arm off the floor. It got to the point where the roof should have been, but his hand kept rising. Soon Sam's arm was pointing straight up, as if he were asking a question in class.

He'd made it to the shaft.

THE SURFACE OF THE ROCK WAS UNEVEN. Sam could imagine Mary's grandfather groping blindly, finding footholds and handholds and climbing up its face. Sam worked that out by touch, but there was no way of knowing how high the climb would be. He reassured himself that it would be as easy as scaling the climbing wall in the school gym, except blindfolded.

Thankfully, it was a short climb. The shaft was only the height of two tall men, but as he followed in Jason Verulam's footsteps, Sam couldn't help but reflect on how terrifying it must have been for the man as he dug for his life. Jason had had to drag boards through the tunnel to shore up the vertical shaft; Sam only had to climb.

When Sam's head hit wood, the collision brought down a light dusting of sand.

It had to be the lid Jason had written about.

Sam gave it a push, but he could tell it was pointless. So he tried the opposite. Wedging his fingers between two of the planks of wood, Sam pulled. A gap opened, and he was rewarded with a mouthful of sand for his troubles. He turned away in surprise. A lucky move, because the lid over the tunnel turned out to be as tired as the rest of the construction.

There was a loud *woompf* as seven or eight pieces of wood, and what felt like just as many tons of sand, plunged behind Sam down the shaft. If he hadn't had his head down, trying to spit out the mouthful of sand he had just swallowed, it would have taken him with it.

Sam looked up. The view was exactly the same. Black. But slowly it began to change. As a gentle breeze wafted across his face, tiny pinpricks of light began to spoil the flat monotone color he had gotten so used to.

IT WAS AN UNDIGNIFIED EXIT. SAM slithered rather than climbed out of the shaft into the small crater that had been created by the opening of the tunnel. As he lay there, the elation at having escaped was dulled by the complete and utter exhaustion that had seeped into every corner of his body. He breathed deeply, keeping his eyes wide open. He knew if he shut them now, he'd be out like a light, and he couldn't afford for that to happen. He had to keep going. He had to get help for his uncle, and fast.

Thanks to Sam's weakened state, there was a time lag between his decision to get to his feet and his body making it happen. In those few seconds the voices reached his ears. Two men arguing.

Sam slid up to the edge of the crater. A few hundred feet away the huge hulk of a giant helicopter was squatting on the sand, pointing directly at Sam's hiding place. The eerie red glow in the cockpit gave away the presence of a pilot busily flicking switches. But the voices belonged to the two men standing beside the helicopter's open side door. It was the Short-Haired Man and his partner with the beard, who had tried to grab Sam at his uncle's apartment.

While his distance from the men gave him some comfort, Sam couldn't help but wish he were close enough to hear what they were arguing about. The man with the beard was doing most of the talking, along with a lot of arm waving and finger pointing. He was worked up about something, and Sam got the impression that the Short-Haired Man was getting a real telling off.

The voices died as another figure loomed out of the darkness from behind the chopper. It was Hadi. There was no sign of the Ark. Sam guessed it had already been loaded, because the bearded man suddenly leapt on board, and the engines roared to life.

The rotors began to spin, and two spotlights above the cockpit cast a road-sized band of light out in front of the helicopter. Sam realized that it was going to head straight for him the moment it left the ground. He shuffled back from the edge of the crater and reached into the shaft for the canvas he had seen stuck to the rim. Jason Verulam had placed it over the wood to stop the sand from seeping in, but now it would have to make do as instant camouflage.

The engines screamed like beasts demanding to be let off their leads. The rotors reached their top speed, sending clouds of sand over the crater. Sam dragged the canvas over him and waited.

The racket grew louder still and it felt like the helicopter, rather than taking off, was simply rolling across the sand toward Sam. Then the chaos passed, the wind dropped, and the roar of the engines began to soften. Sam looked up to see the red flashes of the helicopter's taillights as it cruised out over the desert in a wide arc that brought it back over its landing spot. The spotlights lit up the Short-Haired Man and Hadi sitting next to a small fire that had been blocked from Sam's view when the chopper was on the ground. The lights revealed one more secret lurking out in the darkness: a quad bike.

As the sounds of the helicopter faded away, Sam made plans for his own departure.

25

THE END OF
THE ROAD

THE FIRE'S ORANGE GLOW SILHOUETTED
Hadi and the Short-Haired Man. Calm had returned
to the desert, but with the Ark safely dispatched, there
was nothing to hold them there. They seemed involved
in a discussion, but it was only a matter of time before
they would head for the quad. Sam had to get there
first.

Like the chopper, he moved out in a wide arc that
kept him as far from the fire as possible. Sam waited
until he had the bike between him and the fire before
he zeroed in on its parking spot on a low ridge.
Thankfully, the key was in it. Mounting it silently, Sam

made sure the headlights were off before he turned it on. Just one click, to light up the instrument panel. The bike was in neutral. Another piece of luck.

As Sam pushed the bike down the slope to make his getaway, a commotion at the fire caught his attention.

The Short-Haired Man leapt up. Sam panicked, thinking he'd been spotted, but there was a cry from Hadi as he was hauled to his feet by his collar.

"Up. Get up!" said the Short-Haired Man, loudly enough for Sam to hear.

Hadi sobbed as he rose. "Please, why? What have I done?"

The Short-Haired Man didn't reply. He tossed a small foldable spade at the terrified Egyptian. "Over there," he said, pointing a few feet from the fire. "Start digging."

Hadi stumbled to the spot and began to shovel. "Please, mister . . . I will not tell a soul of what I have seen."

The Short-Haired Man didn't respond. Instead, he pulled a gun from his belt and motioned for Hadi to continue digging. After a few minutes he stepped forward to inspect the work.

"This is nothing personal, boy. People have died for knowing far less than you do." He knocked the shovel from Hadi's hand. "Get in the hole."

It was more of a shallow trench than a hole, and Hadi latched on to this. "No, wait!" he pleaded, scrambling for the shovel. "I can dig more." It was a last desperate attempt to prolong his life.

"Enough!" the Short-Haired Man yelled. His voice echoed out into the desert, reducing Hadi to stifled sobs. "Get down on your knees. I'll make this quick for you."

With a metallic *click* the Short-Haired Man cocked his weapon. He straightened his arm and took aim at the back of Hadi's head. The boy's whimpering died away, but just as his finger tightened on the trigger, the Short-Haired Man was distracted by the sound of his quad bike starting. He looked up the rise, to the spot where he'd parked it. By the time he realized the noise hadn't come from there, it was too late. He spun back toward the fire as Sam roared out of the darkness behind it. Another second and he might have had a chance to get a shot off, but the quad was coming on too fast.

Showers of sparks and embers erupted from both sides of the bike as it crossed the fire and plowed on, and at the very last second Sam adjusted his course by a fraction.

One of the chunky tires clipped the Short-Haired Man, sending him flying back.

Sam skidded to a stop next to Hadi, who was still kneeling in the trench. "Get on now," he said.

Eyes wide with surprise, Hadi leapt out of the trench and onto the bike. Sam kicked it into gear, and they tore off into the night.

"You saved me! You saved me!" shouted Hadi as they sped through the dark. He sounded surprised, and Sam was too. His escape had been assured. With the Short-Haired Man watching Hadi dig his trench, Sam could have raced off into the desert. But once he saw what was going on, he knew he had to act.

It wasn't as if he owed Hadi any favors, but Sam couldn't live with the idea of someone losing his life because he hadn't done anything to help.

Their getaway was interrupted as two quick shots rang out.

Sam felt Hadi tense up and thought the Egyptian had been hit, but the bike was the victim. The engine spluttered and died, and the quad began to lose speed. Before it came to a stop, Hadi leapt from the back.

"Wait! Don't run!" Sam yelled.

Hadi wasn't listening. "Come, come," he urged, moving farther away. "We must go."

Sam slipped off the bike and crouched behind it. Half his brain was screaming, *Run!* The other half said, *Stay put.* Another shot rang out, and Hadi came scuttling back to the bike.

"Get around here," hissed Sam.

The boy slumped down next to him, his head falling on Sam's shoulder. The action seemed out of place till Sam heard the labored breathing.

"Hadi, are you okay?" Sam tried to push him upright, and his hand got covered in something warm and sticky. "What's wrong?" It was a stupid question. Sam knew the answer. He'd been shot.

Hadi's head fell back onto Sam again as he let out a weak groan.

"He should have listened to you, Sam." The voice, mixed with the gentle scuffing of boots on sand, drifted out of the blackness. A few seconds later the slim silhouette of the Short-Haired Man appeared behind the quad, but the night-vision unit covering his face gave his head a bulky inhuman look.

"He's dying. He needs help!" Sam screamed.

"What do you care? He betrayed you."

"He doesn't deserve to die."

"He was a sewer rat working for money," the Short-Haired Man fired back. "And happy to leave you to die in that ship."

"No, he wasn't," said Sam. "That was your idea."

The Short-Haired Man conceded the point with a

shrug of his shoulders. "No matter. Now I have a job for you." He pulled a slim flashlight out of his pocket, and Sam recoiled in horror as its beam lit up Hadi. A red stain covered his entire right shoulder, and it grew as Sam watched.

There was no reaction from the Short–Haired Man. "Bring the boy," he said. He walked off, holding the tiny flashlight behind him like a theater usher. It was a deliberate act, a sign of contempt. His way of showing Sam he didn't see the boy as a threat.

Hadi let out another weak groan as Sam hooked his arms under the boy's shoulders and dragged him away from the bike. Sam's head was spinning from a toxic mix of shock and exhaustion. He knew every step he took was one closer to their deaths, but his mind was blank. He was out of ideas. Out of hope. So he dragged Hadi through the sand one step at a time.

26

FALL GUY

THE MINIATURE BALL OF LIGHT LOOKED like a yellow star sitting low on the horizon. Each time Sam turned to make sure he was on course, it was hovering there in the distance.

If the Short-Haired Man was getting impatient, he didn't show it, remaining silent until Sam reached him. "You know, Sam, when you appeared across the fire on the motorbike, I couldn't quite believe what I was seeing."

His tone betrayed something approaching admiration, but Sam didn't care. As he gently lowered Hadi's body to the ground, he was past caring about anything.

"I will admit," continued the Short-Haired Man, "I was a little confused. I mean, how had you escaped?

And then, on my walk from the fire to the bike, I spotted this." Sam followed the beam of the penlight to the small crater surrounding the tunnel opening. He had been vaguely aware that it was off to his left as he and Hadi had raced away from the fire, but he hadn't been sure of the exact location. Then again, he hadn't had the advantage of night-vision goggles.

"Obviously, you didn't have time to dig this yourself, but the fact that you found it and managed to get out so fast—quite impressive. And now, lucky for you, I think," he added.

"Why?" asked Sam.

"Because the two of you would not have fit in the grave the boy dug." The Short-Haired Man laughed at his own sick joke. "You know, Sam, while I applaud your escape attempt, the pity is, if you had stayed where you were, you might have lived."

Sam couldn't help himself. "What are you talking about?"

"You saw the helicopter, yes?"

"Yes," he admitted. "I also saw your boss chewing you out." Sam couldn't see the Short-Haired Man's face, but he sensed a scowl.

"He is not my boss," he insisted. "We were forced to work together on this mission. It was my employer's wish. Not mine."

"Whatever. Looked like you were getting a lecture to me."

The conversation was pointless; it wouldn't affect how things turned out. But there was a small dose of satisfaction, knowing he'd gotten under his executioner's skin.

"A lecture, you say?" The word was delivered awkwardly. "Actually, no, the discussion was about whether you and your uncle should live or die."

Sam didn't respond, but he was listening intently, and the Short-Haired Man knew it. "That's right, Sam. My *partner*"—he emphasized the word—"insisted that you should both live. He told me he intended to radio in your location to the authorities once I had departed. So you see, if you hadn't tried quite so hard, you would have lived."

"Would have?"

"That's right. You've given me the chance to finish this job the way I wanted to. Now get up and dump the boy down the shaft."

The conversation was over. Sam saw the Short-Haired Man glance at his watch, and as he did, he realized that the darkness was abating. The world was still black, but the shade had lightened just a fraction.

"Why?" asked Sam.

"Why what?" the Short-Haired Man asked impatiently.

"Why did your *boss*"—Sam emphasized the word—"care if we lived or died?"

"Your parents."

"What about them?"

"He said he was doing it for them."

"My parents are dead," said Sam.

"Not according to him."

"What do you mean?" he asked, remembering what Jasper had said.

"I mean, your parents are alive. Now get on with it, or I'll make your death more painful than you can possibly imagine."

Sam didn't hear the Short-Haired Man's threat. His mind was spinning out of control. Could his parents really be alive? As he allowed the thought to linger, he felt a spark deep down inside him. The Short-Haired Man said something else, but Sam was lost in a growing surge of emotion. Finally, the man's raging words sank in.

"Did you hear me?" he roared, his face reddening, a combination of the strain and frustration. Even now, all Sam could manage was a blank stare as the thoughts flooding his mind overpowered his ability to focus on anything else.

The Short-Haired Man grabbed Sam's arm and shoved him toward Hadi's body. The physical contact snapped Sam out of his trance. He looked at the man waving the gun in front of him, then looked down at the boy's body, and he understood. He was useful only for as long as it took to toss Hadi down the shaft. He would be next. Despite the horror of the situation the spark inside him began to glow brighter and warmer. His parents were alive.

He knelt by the body, fumbling awkwardly, as if he were trying to work out how to pick it up.

"You need to use both hands," growled the Short-Haired Man. But Sam couldn't, because he had one hand behind him.

The chunky brass weapon had been tucked into the back of his pants since he'd found it next to the skeleton. It had left deep grooves in his skin, but he didn't feel a thing as he got to his feet and aimed it.

"A flare gun? Really, Sam?"

The Short-Haired Man was so unimpressed by Sam's last roll of the dice, he didn't even bother to raise his own gun. Instead, he laughed. "Let me guess. You found that in the ship and thought you would use it on me when I least expected it?" He shook his head slowly. "It looks old, Sam. And dirty. Think it still works?"

Sam had no idea.

"Pull the trigger. Find out." The Short-Haired Man saw the hesitation in Sam's eyes. "Go on," he screamed. "Do it! It's your last chance, Sam. Pull the trigger!"

Despite the situation Sam couldn't do it, and the Short-Haired Man saw the doubt in his eyes. He lunged for the old flare gun and ripped it from Sam's hand. Aiming it in the air, he pulled the trigger.

There was a dull *thunk*, and the Short-Haired Man laughed. "Did you even check if it was loaded?" he said as he pulled the trigger again.

His laughter drowned out the repeated *thunk*s coming from the gun.

"Not even loaded," the Short-Haired Man said as he inspected the chunky brass gun. "I'm not surprised. This is an antique." He jammed it inside his jacket and grinned at Sam. "Thank you for the parting gift." He was about to say something else but stopped, and Sam watched the look on his face drift from surprise to concern. Then he started smoking.

Thick and white, the smoke belched from the Short-Haired Man's jacket, and he began to scream. The noise was fueled by shock, pain, and anger. He had been wrong about the flare gun—it had been loaded, but the shell was old and corroded. A few pulls of the trigger had been needed to set it off, and the Short-Haired Man had gladly obliged.

Fat red tongues of flame signaled the second stage of an explosion that was meant to happen hundreds of feet up in the air. The Short-Haired Man was transformed into a fiery ball of flailing arms and legs as he charged toward Sam.

A quick sidestep would have gotten him out of trouble, but Sam was way past being able to summon the strength for that kind of move. So, he did the only thing he could manage and dropped to the ground.

Instead of hitting Sam, the Short-Haired Man hit a human speed bump crouched right on the edge of the small crater, and for a fraction of a second the brightly burning flare did fly through the air. Then there was the sickening *thump* of a body landing at the bottom of the shaft.

SEARING PAIN SHOT THROUGH SAM'S SIDE as he tried to stand, but a couple of cracked ribs was a better outcome than the one he had been staring in the face a few seconds earlier.

Smoke billowed out of the tunnel opening as he stepped down into the crater. The night sky had morphed to a dark blue in the past few eventful minutes. It was still too dark to see to the bottom of the shaft, but the dull moans drifting up with the smoke told Sam the Short-Haired Man still lived. "Can you hear me?" he called out. "I can help you." The moaning stopped, but there was no response. "I can help you," repeated Sam. "But first you have to tell me something. . . . How did that man know my parents are alive?"

There was no answer. Sam began to think the fall had become fatal, but then a tortured growl erupted from the smoky pit, and the Short-Haired Man spoke.

"I don't . . . I don't even know who he was. I told you, my employers made me work with him."

"Then tell me who your employers are. If you don't, I'll leave you down there to die."

"If I tell you who they are," muttered the Short-Haired Man, "I'll die anyway."

The distant thumping sound drew Sam's attention away from the shaft. He turned and scanned the horizon. Help at last? Or more trouble? Not that it would affect what Sam did. He had nothing left. All he could do was watch and wait.

It had been getting harder and harder to fight off the exhaustion. It came in waves, each stronger than the last and carrying the tantalizing promise of relief from the tortured state he was in. Sleep was just a heartbeat away. All he had to do was close his eyes.

Dawn was breaking. Soon the sun would arrive to claim its throne over Egypt for another day, but the helicopter would reach Sam first. The noise grew louder, and then, through weary eyes, he saw the chopper appear out of the blue-black haze, the Verulam family logo emblazoned across the nose.

Sam went down hard. The slope of the crater broke his fall, but the panic hit him like a freight train. Twisting his body, he looked down as the first rays of the new day lit up a hand from hell.

Five bloody, burn-ravaged fingers were locked around his ankle. The climb up the rock wall must have taken superhuman strength, but what Sam saw now, hovering in the white smoke coming out of the shaft, was barely recognizable as human—a burnt and swollen head coated in sand made wet by the weeping skin.

"Come here," the melting beast raged. "Die with me, Sam."

Sam kicked at the hand with his free leg, and then drove the heel of his boot down onto the fingers, but he couldn't stop the slide into the hole.

Globs of red-tinged saliva flew out of the smoke as the horror show that had been the Short-Haired Man continued to moan. "Come to me."

Sam was being pulled over the edge of the shaft. In one last attempt to stop himself, he threw both hands behind him and dug his fingers into the side of the crater. All he ended up with were two big handfuls of sand, which he threw at the two small, dark pools staring at him through the smoke.

The Short-Haired Man didn't let go of Sam, but he pulled his head back in shock as the sand hit his eyes. That movement made him lose his handhold on the rock, and he fell back, smashing into the fragile wooden wall. After seventy-three years Jason Verulam's escape tunnel had finally had enough. Bone-dry wood cracked and gave way. A muffled cry was quickly drowned out by the roar of a desert, hungry to reclaim the space it had been denied for so long.

Sam, with his legs hanging over the shaft, could only lie back and cover his face as a fountainlike blast of sandy air erupted into the sky.

27

PAST, PRESENT, FUTURE

SAM HEARD RAISED VOICES BEHIND HIM.
Hadi had been found. Someone was calling for medics.
He tried to sit up, but the sting of his broken ribs forced
him back onto the sand, which was already warming
in the early morning sun.

"You look relaxed," said Mary as she sat down next
to Sam.

"I'm pretending I'm sunbathing at the Cairo
Waterpark," Sam answered. "How's Hadi?"

"The medics say he's lost a lot of blood. They're
going to chopper him to a hospital right away." Mary

began brushing away the sand that had covered Sam when the shaft imploded. "Who is he?"

Sam was about to reply when the image of his uncle passed out down in the *Panehesy* flooded back into his mind. "Jasper! We've got to get him out!"

"It's okay, Sam," Mary assured him. "That's being taken care of too. You hear that?"

It was the repetitive thumping of another approaching chopper. "A rescue team is almost here."

"Let me guess. Bassem knew some people?"

"Actually, it was my father who arranged it."

"How did you find me?"

"We picked up a radio report from a helicopter to the police," explained Mary. "Bassem persuaded them to let us handle the situation."

"That chopper had the Ark in it," said Sam. "Uncle Jasper found it, but now it's gone."

"That doesn't matter right now, Sam. What matters is that you're okay and that you found your uncle. But how did you get out? The man on the radio said you were trapped underground."

Sam pointed at the shallow hole his legs were hanging over. "This was the exit of a tunnel . . . that your grandfather dug."

Sam told Mary everything he'd learned from his

uncle and from Jason Verulam's journal. As he spoke, there was something in the way she accepted the information that made Sam think Mary already knew some of what he was talking about.

"Well, the first thing we need to do is get you out of here," Mary said when Sam had finished. "Do you think you can walk?"

Sam nodded. "With a bit of help."

The only evidence of the shaft's existence was the wooden frame that Sam's legs were draped over. His pants had caught on a splinter, and as Mary pulled them free, the frame gave way with a *crack*. More sand poured into the hole, and with it, a faded piece of paper that went unnoticed by Sam and Mary as they climbed out of the crater.

AN INJECTION HAD DULLED THE PAIN IN Sam's side, but it was a long and agonizing wait as the rescue team dug their way back into the *Panehesy* through the smokestack. With the mess from the explosion cleared, men and medical equipment were ferried into the buried ship, and all Sam could do was sit and wait. Mary did her best to distract him with food, drink, and cheerful banter, but his eyes remained fixed on the small portable crane that had been set up over the new hole.

The sun was directly overhead when the signal came that Jasper was being brought out.

"Sam, wait here," Mary said as he struggled to his feet. It was sound advice. Despite the painkillers, the throbbing around his cracked ribs was almost unbearable. But the urge to see his uncle was stronger, and he pushed through the cluster of men in red jumpsuits.

Jasper slid out of the top of the *Panehesy*'s smoke-stack strapped to a lightweight metal rescue stretcher. He blinked uncomfortably as the sun hit his eyes, but was unable to lift an arm to shield them. A medic spotted the problem and stepped in to block the light, and it was then Jasper caught sight of Sam.

"My boy, my boy," he exclaimed. "They told me you were okay."

"I'm fine," said Sam, beaming. "I was worried about you."

"Me?" asked Jasper, with a look of mock surprise. "I went into the *Panehesy* down a rope by hand. I've come out business class."

"And you don't even have a big bum," quipped Sam. His uncle didn't get it, but behind Sam, Mary laughed. "Uncle Jasper, I want you to meet Mary. Mary Verulam," he said as Mary crouched down next to the stretcher.

"Hello, Mr. Force."

Jasper nodded approvingly. "Delighted to meet you, Mary, and please call me Jasper."

"I'm glad you're okay, Jasper," said Mary. "And I know my father will be very relieved as well."

The reunion was cut short as the men in the red jumpsuits, who had been standing back politely, muscled in and took control of their patient. They carried him to the back of their chopper, which was set up like a small hospital room. It was made clear to Sam and Mary that their presence was not welcomed while the medics did their work, so the two of them sat in the shade of the Verulam chopper and watched.

"What's Bassem doing?" Sam asked. He'd seen the giant Egyptian take a couple of the rescue team and some equipment over to what was left of Jason Verulam's tunnel.

"I think they're planning to dig out the body," said Mary. "My father will want to find out as much as he can about that man who tailed you here." She got to her feet. "You wanna come check it out?"

Sam shook his head.

"I've had enough digging in the sand for one day."

THE MEN IN RED CONTINUED TO FUSS over Uncle Jasper until one of them finally signaled to Sam that he was allowed to approach.

"Your uncle is stabilized, but he's lost a lot of blood," Sam was informed by one of the medics. "We need to get him to a hospital, so you must say your good-byes quickly."

Jasper had been sedated, and his glassy eyes watched Sam approach from under sagging eyelids. "I'm so sorry about all this," he said, reaching out for his nephew. "I failed you."

"What do you mean?" asked Sam.

"I was led to believe we might find something to tell us what happened to your parents, but it seems to have been a dead end."

"Maybe, maybe not," said Sam. "Anyway, I'm the one who should be apologizing. I led those men to you. Because of me, they got the Ark."

"I don't think they did," announced Mary as she joined Sam at the door of the chopper. Look what Bassem just found." She held up the faded pieces of paper. "It was jammed into the frame at the mouth of the tunnel."

"What is it?" asked Sam.

"A letter from my grandfather."

June 25 1942

I have freed myself from the iron tomb of Panehesy but find I have ascended from one black world to another. I cannot wait for night to pass. I am close to death and must have water. The Nile was beneath us before the storm; it cannot be far. From there I can begin my trek to Al Minya.

This is my plan, but should I not prevail, this letter must serve to record what I am unable to pass on. I leave it in the hope it will find its way to those worthy of it.

I have seen the original Ark. Engraved on it is the record of a time when there were many. Many Arks in many pyramids across the world. The Arks were destroyed; the pyramids left as empty shells. Why?

Recorded also was the location of a pyramid that this Ark can rest in. P518 is carrying this sacred treasure, sacred heart, to its new home.

P518 was my grand deception. It will complete the mission while I was supposed to accompany the decoy. I had thought I was the only one on board who knew of this plan until Thomas's confession.

His death weighs heavily on my conscience. I have killed before in the name of our sacred task, and if called upon, I will kill again. But I pray I shall never be forced to commit an act so horrific as that which I perpetrated on the traitor, Thomas.

Surely no man can commit a crime so heinous as to feed upon another. But without his blood to sustain me I would never have made it out of the Panehesy. I will tell myself the end justifies the means, but this rings hollow within my soul.

I leave now with the knowledge that I shall be brought to account for this vile act. In this life, or the next.

Jason K. Verulam

"He must have gone the wrong way," said Sam when Mary had finished reading the note to them. He glanced down toward the Nile, blue and sparkling in the midday sun. "The river's only a couple hundred meters away."

"That's true," said Jasper. "But it was night; he was

near death. I guess he mistakenly stumbled off into the desert. . . ."

Mary stared at the letter as if she hoped it would give up a few more clues. "No wonder he went crazy." She sighed. "He was racked with guilt because he drank human blood to survive."

"Incredible," said Jasper. "The will to survive . . . the effort his escape must have taken . . . Makes ours seem like a bit of a picnic, eh, Sam?"

Sam laughed. "Speak for yourself."

"But you know what this means?" continued Jasper. "Thanks to Mary's grandfather, the original Ark got away safely, and P518 is the key. . . . If we only knew exactly what it was and where it was headed."

"P518." Mary recited it slowly. "It was engraved on my grandfather's arm. Maybe he did it when his mind started to go. So he wouldn't forget." She shuddered. "It used to gross me out. He must have done it himself, out here in the desert. It looked disgusting. These big purple scars on his forearm. Whenever I went to see him, he was just lying there, rubbing them like they were braille."

"But you never knew what they were?" asked Sam.

"No. Neither did my father, until five years ago." Mary looked at Sam, then his uncle. "Jasper, I'm afraid my father wasn't entirely straight with you about your mission to hunt down the *Panehesy*."

Jasper's hairy eyebrows lifted. "Really? How so?"

Mary threw Sam another embarrassed look before she spoke. "I don't think he thought you would find out any more about Sam's parents out here. You have to understand," she pleaded, "he's obsessed with his work to uncover the secret behind the pyramids. He would have said anything to get you to help him."

"I see," said Jasper.

"But he did have some information that he told me he intended to share with you. Father always suspected that P518 was an important clue. He created a computer program to scan the Internet for anything to do with it." Mary removed her phone from her pocket and pulled up a page. "When he found this five years ago, he knew it was something to do with my grandfather's pyramid theory." Mary handed the phone to Jasper, who propped himself up on his stretcher.

"That is the story that led my father to get in touch with your parents five years ago, Sam," Mary said. "He knew submarine *P518* had to be linked to my grandfather's original mission, and he saw a chance to solve the mystery. My father was aware of your parents' interest in the links between the pyramids around the world, so he offered them the chance to go to Belize and investigate the submarine."

"They told Jasper they were in Jamaica," Sam said.

STORM UNCOVERS SUB BURIED IN RIVERBANK

POLICEMAN FINDS WWII SUB BURIED IN RIVERBANK

A mystery, hidden in river mud for nearly seventy years, was uncovered recently. The discovery of the World War II submarine was announced by Felix Ramos, head of the Orange Walk Police Department, at a press conference yesterday. Officials say there are no records of the submarine in Belize in World War II, and they are

mystified by the discovery. Superintendent Ramos said that a cal-
endar found on board dates the sub's arrival to 1942. Experts were
also surprised by the location of the sub, saying it was incredible that
the vessel made it so far up the New River. Superintendent Ramos
said the submarine had been hidden in a small side stream near
the ruins of Lamanai. Had it not been for the recent typhoon that
washed away large sections of the riverbank, it would have remained
undiscovered.

Mary nodded. "My father swore them to secrecy
and insisted they tell no one."

"And then they disappeared," Jasper said as he handed
Mary's phone back.

Mary nodded. "My father felt terrible about that,"
she said. "He told me he spent thousands sending inves-
tigators to Belize to find out what happened to them,
but there was no trace."

"But they were onto something," Sam said. "Your
grandfather's last letter proves it."

Jasper lay back on his stretcher. "It does indeed
appear that the next clue to this ancient mystery leads
us to Belize," he mumbled as he closed his eyes.

MARY AND SAM KEPT THEIR HEADS DOWN
until the wind and sand settled. Sam felt uncomfortable
about being separated from his uncle so soon. It was a

strange, new feeling. So little of the past week had been spent with him, but still Sam felt a new bond brought on by the adventure they had both been part of.

"So, what now, Sam Force?" Mary asked as they watched the rescue chopper drift down the Nile toward Al Minya.

Sam shrugged his shoulders. "Uncle Jasper believes in the pyramid network. He's keen to get to Belize."

"Well, I know my father would be more than happy to have another believer on his books."

"How about two?" asked Sam.

"You're going to need my help."

"You can start now. Where is Belize?"

Mary laughed. "Central America. Don't worry, I'll get you some books. But I'll make sure they're nice little ones, because I know how you hate to study."

"Think your dad would spring for business class?"

"Probably not. Your bum isn't big enough."

Sam smiled. He was still staring at the Nile, but his mind was already thousands of miles away. His uncle had been right: The clues to the ancient mystery of the pyramid network led to Belize. But someone out there was hunting the same prize, and they would all be in danger. Sam also knew that those people held the answers to the other mystery. He hadn't said anything about the Short-Haired Man's claims that his parents were still alive. Not to Jasper or to Mary. He would, of course, but he needed time to himself. Time to get his head around the implications. A trip to Belize was definitely in the cards. But it would be about far more than hunting for a pyramid.

THE END . . . OF THE BEGINNING.

ACKNOWLEDGMENTS

LIKE BUILDING A PYRAMID, IT TOOK MANY people to construct this book. The foundations were laid when the real-life Jasper Force, a seven-year-old obsessed with all things Egyptian, told me a strange fact about Ra the sun god. My thanks and some Moroccan mint tea must go to my good friend Gary Herbert for acting as my sounding board and critic in the shisha cafés of Abu Dhabi. To my favorite Iranian, Mo Aram, thanks for being Sam's artistic hand and good luck with designing that glowing dress for Beyoncé. I also owe a Pharaoh's ransom in thank-you's to my agent, Mandy Hubbard, for believing in this story from the start, and Michael Strother at Aladdin for his enthusiasm and guidance as the book came to life. Finally, my love and gratitude goes to the two ladies at the center of my universe—my daughter, Frankie, and my wife, Kirsty. I love the friends I have gathered on this thin raft—especially you two.

The hunt continues . . . in Belize!
Read an excerpt from

SAM BROKE OUT IN A SWEAT AS ALL EYES
turned in his direction. Behind him, he heard Andrew
Fletcher snickering. They hadn't been friends since
Sam beat him to a spot on the four-man rowing team.

"I said come here, Force."

Mr. Stevenson's voice filled the classroom, and yet
he hadn't seemed to speak very loud at all. Sam got
to his feet, wondering if voice projection was a skill
they taught at teachers college. He pushed in his chair,
taking care not to scrape the legs on the floor. It was
one of Mr. Stevenson's pet peeves. No point in making
the situation worse than it already was.

Mr. Stevenson watched Sam approach, holding the

note distastefully between two fingers. He waved it in the direction of the nervous junior who had delivered the message. The boy understood the meaning and scuttled for the door.

As Sam got to the front row, Mr. Stevenson screwed up the piece of paper and tossed it into the wire basket in the corner of the room. It was a good shot, no rim. Sam hoped the mutterings of appreciation breaking out around the room might be enough to snap the teacher out of his foul mood. But they weren't.

"Settle down," Mr. Stevenson growled. "If you are not Mr. Force, then you should be attempting this!" He waved the black marker in his other hand at the algebra equation scrawled across the whiteboard.

"But you, Mr. Force, have been summoned to the headmaster's office."

Sam heard Andrew Fletcher mutter something from the back of the class.

"An urgent matter, no doubt. Can you think of anything important enough to warrant the interruption of your lesson in Advanced Algebra?"

Sam assumed he wasn't meant to reply, but he could think of hundreds of reasons to interrupt Advanced Algebra. For him, math ranked even higher than bathroom cleaning on his list of hated tasks at his boarding school.

"Well?" Mr. Stevenson pointed the marker at Sam accusingly.

"No, sir," Sam replied.

For a moment the man regarded him with the same look he'd given the headmaster's note, then he jabbed his marker at the door. "Off you go, then."

As Sam left the room, Mr. Stevenson spoke again, loud enough for everyone to hear.

"You'll have a lot to catch up on, Mr. Force. See Mr. Fletcher this evening. He can take you through the work you've missed."

Sam grinned as he heard Andrew Fletcher's muttered protests. He wouldn't make a very good study partner, but it served him right. As Sam walked down the deserted corridor, he reflected on his teacher's words. Mr. Stevenson was right. You weren't called for during class unless it was very important. So what was he walking into?

THE LONG OAK BENCH CREAKED AS SAM sat down. Looking around the office, with its floor-to-ceiling oak panels, old paintings, and grandfather clock, Sam realized that nearly everything in the place was creaky. That included Miss Ingle, the headmaster's secretary. According to one of the boarders, whose older brother had also attended St. Albans, Miss Ingle had been at the school since it was founded. Sam didn't think that was possible. It would mean she was . . . He couldn't work it out—maybe he could have if he'd paid more attention in algebra—but he knew it would make her very old.

St. Albans was a grand school, if you were into that sort of thing. Huge old oaks and big stone buildings covered with moss dotted a well-manicured lawn. Sam thought it belonged in England, fifty years ago, not modern-day Boston. Not that Sam had ever been to an English boarding school. He could hardly remember anything about England. His last trip to that country had been over five years ago, before his parents died. No, not died, he corrected himself—disappeared.

Five years ago, Sam's life changed forever when his parents were murdered. He'd been left to spend summer vacations in Cairo, with his Uncle Jasper, and the rest of the year at St. Albans School for Boys.

But in July, everything changed again. In just a few days he had uncovered a conspiracy involving pyramids around the world and the famous Ark of the Covenant. He had learned his parents were involved, but more important for Sam, he'd been given hope that they were alive. His world had turned upside down, but almost as quickly as it had changed, he'd had to go back to being a schoolkid. It was impossible. Not with what he knew.

After his Egyptian adventure, he'd been desperate to keep going, to stay on the trail of his parents. But days had passed by with no progress. His uncle convinced him to return to Boston—a temporary situation, he had promised Sam, until he was able to get the appropriate resources in place. That had been six long weeks ago. Even Mary, who had been so keen to help him solve the mystery of his parents and the secret behind a world-wide network of pyramids, had lost interest. After Sam had returned to Boston, they had been in touch almost every day via e-mail, as they researched the information they had uncovered in Egypt. But in the last couple of weeks, things had changed. Her messages were less frequent, and the subject matter had become routine stuff about school and music. It was as if she had put their adventure behind her and moved on.

But Sam couldn't. Not while there was still hope his parents were alive.

Sam had a nagging feeling that his summons to the headmaster's office was to do with the events in Egypt. Since his return, he hadn't felt the same about anything, especially schoolwork. His grades were dropping almost as fast as his bangs. And both had become a source of tension.

St. Albans liked its boys' hair to look as well-groomed as its lawns, and both were cut often. Sam's hair had already grown beyond an acceptable length when he returned from Egypt. It had been one of the first things the head teacher had commented on: "Be sure you're front of the line when the barber visits this weekend, Force," he had commanded. After that, it had become a thing for Sam.

He found an excuse to miss the barber's school visit that weekend, and the next visit, a few weeks later. In the outside world, Sam's hair would not have even received a second glance, but within the pristine walls of St. Albans he began to turn heads. It was a small thing, but to Sam it had become a symbol of defiance. A personal reminder that he didn't belong there anymore. Not when there were so many unanswered questions waiting for him in the outside world.

By the time the door to the headmaster's office opened, Sam had prepared himself for a showdown about his hair. So he was totally unprepared when the two men inside greeted him with a round of applause.

The headmaster was clapping politely, but the man beside him looked like he was about to cry with joy as he slapped his small hands together so fast they were a pink blur. He was a short man, but anyone looked short next to the towering Mr. Billington, St. Albans's headmaster.

"Come in Sam, have a seat," Mr. Billington said. He immediately sat down, looking relieved to have an excuse to stop clapping.

Sam eyed the chair in front of him, but the short man darted forward, gripped his hand, and started shaking it with the same energy he'd put into his clapping.

"Mr. Force, St. Albans's best-kept secret, I think. How very, very exciting."

Very confusing, more like it, Sam thought as he watched his hand being pumped up and down. The man spoke with an accent, and something about him was familiar. Then Sam placed it. He was St. Albans's music teacher, Mr. *Ber*-something.

"Mr. Beroduchi has just received an e-mail informing us of your success, Sam," the headmaster said, holding up a printout. At the top, Sam saw an old-fashioned logo.

"Yes, yes," said the overexcited music teacher. He reached across the desk, grabbed the e-mail from the headmaster's hand, and waved it triumphantly in Sam's face. "My dear boy. Why did you keep your talent from me . . ." He glanced at the e-mail. "Well, no, this explains why. But, my boy, I can't tell you how excited I am to find a pupil with an interest in opera."

Sam had no idea what was going on. He studied the hyped-up music teacher, then the headmaster, searching for a sign that it was a stupid joke, but Mr. Beroduchi interpreted the look in a totally different way.

"Come now, Sam, the time for modesty is over. Now that you have fulfilled your dream."

"My dream?"

"Yes, Sam." The music teacher waved the e-mail in the air again. "Your acceptance into the Shonestein Opera Academy Scholarship Program."

The headmaster cleared his throat to get Sam's and the music teacher's attention. "Come now, Mr. Beroduchi." He motioned to the chairs in front of this desk. "Why don't we give Sam a chance to collect his thoughts. He must be overwhelmed by the news."

"Overwhelmed" wasn't the word. "Freaked-out" was more accurate. Sam sat, and the beaming music teacher pulled his chair close to Sam and continued his excited chatter.

"When I first read the e-mail, I was shocked, to say the least. I had given up hope of finding a student who has my passion for the art of opera. Don't worry, my boy." The teacher thumped Sam's shoulder with the same force he had put into his handshake. "The e-mail mentioned your reluctance to make your love of opera known."

"It did?"

"Yes," the teacher replied. "Your concern that you

might not be good enough. Your desire to prove to yourself that you can compete on the world stage, by submitting an audition to Shonestein's Scholarship Program." The beaming teacher eased up on the shoulder patting as he turned to the headmaster. "We must share this good news with the school, Mr. Billington."

"Yes, we must do that," the headmaster agreed. Sam could see Mr. Billington wasn't as swept up in the moment as the music teacher. Fair enough. Opera? Wasn't that something fat old men did? There was a good reason Sam hadn't recognized Mr. Beroduchi straight away. In his time at St. Albans, Sam had had nothing to do with the music department. He had zero interest in learning anything musical, and, until that moment, the music department had shown zero interest in him.

"Perhaps, Mr. Billington," the music teacher said, "we could entice Sam to give us a performance before his departure."

Sam's mouth dropped, and his mind scrambled, but before he could form the most basic excuse, the headmaster stepped in.

"Regrettably, that won't be possible. Mr. Force is required to leave this evening."

"Ah yes, of course," said Mr. Beroduchi.

"This evening? Where?" asked Sam.

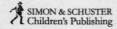